GABRIEL

WINCHESTER BROTHERS BOOK 2

KATHI S. BARTON

This is a work of fiction. Names, characters, places, and incidents are products of the author's imagination or are used fictitiously and are not to be construed as real. Any resemblance to actual events, locations, organizations, or persons, living or dead, is entirely coincidental.

World Castle Publishing, LLC
Pensacola, Florida

Copyright © Kathi S. Barton 2017
Paperback ISBN: 9781629897356
eBook ISBN: 9781629897363
First Edition World Castle Publishing, LLC, July 10, 2017
http://www.worldcastlepublishing.com

Licensing Notes

Cover: Karen Fuller
Editor: Maxine Bringenberg

Prologue

Gabe sat on the grass and watched the kids playing. He'd thought about joining them, but that wasn't his way. He was more likely to wait for one of them to get hurt, because someone always did. He was going to be a doctor when he grew up, he was sure of it. But at sixteen, he knew he had a long way to go until that happened.

Gabe glanced over when he felt someone near, and smiled at Tyler. Tyler would be the person to join the kids, so Gabe was surprised when he didn't.

"Maggie Morehouse, do you know her?" Gabe said that he only knew her by name. "She was killed yesterday. Some idiot pulled her into the woods and killed her. I heard Mom and Dad talking about it this morning."

"Do they know who did it?" Tyler shrugged and Gabe turned to look at the kids in the pond. "I keep waiting on one of them to fall off the big rock and bash their head. I don't know why humans are so dumb when it comes to checking things out before they leap."

"Do you suppose that they have any idea that there are a couple of wolves watching them, a bear, and a cat? Or that any or all of them could run them down, kill them, then run off so's no one will ever find them?" Gabe said he doubted that they even knew they were trespassing. "Mr. Cartwright, he'd sure be all over them if he knew they were here."

Gabe pointed to the line of trees just in front of them. "He's been sitting there watching them since I came up here. I think he just likes watching them have fun. Or like me, he's waiting for one of them to be hurt."

"He told me last week that you were going to amount to something. I told him that I'd already figured that out on my own." Gabe thanked his little brother. "You're welcome. Do you think I might too? Amount to something, I mean?"

"I don't see why not. I mean, we all have to go to college. Don't know how Mom and Dad are going to manage that, but they sure are pushing us. You should think on it now what you want to be. So when the times comes for you to go, you'll have a better idea." Tyler nodded. "Do you know what it is you want to be?"

"Yes, I was thinking on being a cop." Gabe nodded. He'd be a good cop, the way he seemed to be able to read people. "Or a lawyer. I don't know about that so much. Mom and Dad sure think they're an odd bunch."

"You have some time. Just figure it out, like I said, and you'll be good at whatever it is." He looked at the kids again when he heard screaming. He knew someone was in pain, but he wasn't going to save them, not from their own parents. The switch going through the air and smacking hard against their bare skin was funny. "Tyler, someday I'd like to be able to find me a mate, and make her the happiest person in all the world. I talked to Mr. Cartwright about how to make a mate happy, and he said it was all in how you presented yourself. Honesty, he said, was the first step."

"Are there a lot of steps, you think?" He told Tyler there were ten and he was learning them all. "Ten steps to make a girl like you? Sounds like too much work. And if she's already your mate, what do you care if you make her happy or not? Girls are just plain dumb if you ask me."

They were headed back to the house when he thought of the rest of the rules from Mr. Cartwright. There were ten, but they didn't seem all that difficult. He'd made sure to memorize each one, and remembered that with each rule there was a counter rule. Gabe didn't know those. Mr. Cartwright told him those changed with the situation. Like if the woman was nice, headstrong, or just plain stubborn. He hoped she was the first, like his mom.

The house that they lived in wasn't small, but it sure was crowded when they sat down to dinner, and Mr. Cartwright coming over made it a bit tighter. But he'd not change it for the world. He loved the old man like he was his grandda, and he had the best advice when Gabe asked him for it. Smiling, he thought of the dinner that they'd be having tonight. His favorite. Pork chops on the grill with cheesy potatoes, and green beans from the garden.

The pork chops had come their way by a gift card from the local grocery store. They'd been having monthly drawings for people that brought in their own bags and helped with the recycling bins. He had been working in the store for nearly three months now, and his momma had won the thing four times. He thought that she was the only person that brought in her own bags, but it was more because she could carry the extra weight that her large bags would hold rather than the flimsy plastic ones.

As soon as he entered the house he could see the tension in his parents. Mr. Cartwright was sitting at the table drinking a cup of tea and his mom was wiping down the clean counter. His dad was leaning against the wall, but he was far from relaxed.

"Something going on?" They all turned to him and he backed up. "What's happened? I've not been around today, but I might have left something undone."

"It's not you, son. We heard from the pack master. Daniel was saying that that young woman that was killed yesterday, she was murdered by a pair of wolves." Gabe sat down and thought of all the things that could go wrong with that knowledge. His mom continued as she rubbed harder on the surface. "They know who it was…they were a part of our pack, and the pack is going to deal with them."

He knew what she meant, how they would be dealt with, as well as what would happen to their families if they had any. Daniel was a good man, a good leader, and wouldn't kill the families as most would. But they would be turned out. Having no pack would be hard on a person. They were what kept you safe and full when things were rough.

Later that night, he was sitting in the window just looking out when he saw the fires. Gabe watched them for ten minutes while trying not to think of what it meant. Caleb asked him if he was all right.

"I don't know what to think. But I believe that they're burning their homes down with all their things inside. Both of those families had nothing to do with the murders, and now they have nowhere to go." Caleb got out of the bed and came to sit in the other window. "That's not right. I can't believe sometimes that we belong to a place where rules like this are enforced."

"The Zenick family was harboring their uncle. He'd even bragged to them about how he'd killed the woman, yet none of them raised a hand to help Daniel figure it out. They didn't tell him anything until he commanded them to." Gabe hadn't heard that and told his brother so. "The Daltons knew as well. One of the boys even filmed the rape and murder of the woman so they could see where they'd made mistakes and could do better the next time. And they had that planned as well. Their plan was to take two women, one of them pack."

He looked out the window, then at his brother, when something occurred to him. "Mom? Or Alisha?" The pack bitch, Caleb told him. "I had no idea. I wonder why Daniel didn't kill them too?"

"Because he's a good man." Gabe nodded, but said nothing else as Caleb continued. "I don't know that I'd have been able to do that, let them live. To have your family ripped from you the way that they did would be hard to live through."

"When I have a mate, I'm going to make sure that I protect her with all that I am." Caleb asked him what if she was stronger than him. "Nah, I'm going to be her protector. And her mate. She'll be delicate and soft, like Mom is."

"Mom is neither of those things. She's wonderful, but you get her upset and she'd bash your head in with a bat and not think a thing about it." There was that. "She's a wonderful mom, but I sure don't see her as delicate or soft. And I don't know if I'd tell her that either."

Gabe went to bed. He thought about what his brother had said, and wondered if he knew what he was talking about.

9

Even if their mom was a little tense when she was upset, he wasn't going to give his mate any reason to be mad at him. Gabe was going to be the perfect mate to his little flower.

Chapter 1

Gabe was painting the walls in one of his new examination rooms when his dad, who'd been popping in and out over the last three days, said his name. Gabe turned and smiled at him. Dad had on his jeans and T-shirt, like he was ready and able to get going. Alexander, Quinn's dad, was with him.

"We're ready and willing to help you spruce this place up. I heard that you got some of them pretty borders, too, that is going to go up." He said that he had some that were for the children's examining rooms. "To tell you the truth, I'm not sure I'd be any good at that. Alex here, he said he can do that part. I can do a brush or roller."

Gabe set his dad up with not just a paint can and brush, but everything he'd need. The carpets were new and covered with cardboard, so he wasn't worried about that. This room was going to be green, a pale shade that Quinn had helped him pick out.

"If you get tired of painting, I have some equipment that needs to be put together. And since I'm using it on patients,

11

I'd rather you read the instructions and not do it on your own." His dad just glared. "Yeah, I thought you'd feel that way. I'll be in the other room putting together some of the things I got last week."

He was having fun. It had been hard work getting the building ready, but he really was enjoying it. Yesterday he'd received his buyout money from the firm he'd worked for, along with a letter telling him they hoped he failed. Not that wording exactly, but it had been close enough. It had taken him the better part of a day to get over how it had hurt him. Then his first shipment of equipment had arrived and he'd forgotten about them in favor of doing what he enjoyed, being a doctor of his own practice.

There wasn't much to do, not really. He was going to start slowly and work his way up to getting his own patients. There were a couple that had followed him from the firm he'd worked for, but he knew that as soon as he got things running, he'd be busy. Or at least he hoped so. But having the funds to take his time in this had made him sleep better at night.

"Gabriel, come here." He heard the panic in his dad's voice and dropped everything to go see what had happened. Several things popped into his head at once, but when he entered the room, he stood there for several seconds while he let it sink in. "Gabe, this here little fella needs you."

He nodded, but hadn't moved. The little girl holding the cat looked up at him, and he swore that for some reason she wasn't impressed with him. When she lifted the cat up higher in her arms, he started forward to help her when the cat growled.

"He's hurting really, really bad." Gabe said he could see that. "You gotta help him, mister. I just found him, and

Momma don't know that I got him yet. She's going to be powerful mad at me when she finds out, and even madder if he dies. She sure does take on when something dies."

"She's not a he, she's a she." The girl frowned at him. "It's a girl, not a boy cat. And I think.... Why don't you let me take her from you, and I'll see what I can do for her?"

Gabe knew that the cat wasn't going to be happy with him. A wolf and a cat didn't really get along all that well. But he thought if he could get her to come with him without too much pain, he might win her over. As soon as he had the cat in his arms, he saw the little girl's.

"I don't think he was happy about me helping him. It's what's gonna make Momma mad at me. How he scratched me all up." He told her to come along with him, and that it was a girl, not a boy, again. "Momma don't like cats. She said to me that they think they know it all and don't care who knows it. When I saw him...her suffering, I had to do something. Even if he...she didn't like it. Are you sure she's a she?"

"Yes, very much so. I was trained on how to tell the difference." She looked at him like she still wasn't sure. "My dad is going to take the cat into the examining room, and how about I have a look at your arms? Those scratches are pretty deep."

"I guess so, but if he hurts her, then I'm gonna be pretty upset. Not like my momma can be. My grandda used to say she could peel paint off a barn with her tongue. I've never seen her do that, but she can cuss like it's her job." He asked her what her name is. "I don't know you. I'm not supposed to give that stuff out unless my momma says it's okay. You could ask her, I guess, but I'd like for you to make sure that my cat is gonna be all right."

13

"She will be." He cleaned her wounds, all he could do for the child since she wasn't a patient of his, nor did he have permission to stitch up the places where they were really deep. After setting her up with his mom, who had come by to see how things were going, he went to check on the cat. His dad was petting her, but it wasn't making her happy. "How is she?"

"In labor, if I don't miss my bet." He said that she was. "Probably the only reason that we can touch her. She's hurting too much to give us what for."

"The little girl, she hasn't told me her name. Can you find out who she is? And her mom? I'll take care of my very first patient." Not exactly what he wanted to do today, but it was better than painting, he supposed. "Hey, little lady. Let's see what we can do to make you a momma."

In two hours he had helped six kittens come into the world by standing back and watching. And Momma was doing a good job in not tearing him up again. The first few minutes after her delivering her first baby, she'd gotten a little pissed off when he reached in to help. He decided that she knew what she was doing and waited for her to need him. When she seemed to be satisfied, he reached into the little box and petted her.

"You did a great job there, missus. Not my usual patient, but I didn't mind." He pulled out his phone and took several pictures. "If you don't mind, I'm going to hang your picture in my office as my first baby delivery, as well as my first patient."

"You usually talk to animals?" He turned and looked at the woman standing there. "My name is Goldie James. My daughter, Sandy, she's the one that brought you your first

14

delivery."

She was huge with child, and he smiled at her. "It was all right. I didn't stitch her up, and she was very good about not telling me any personal information." Goldie smiled and rubbed her belly. "When are you due?"

"A month. I'm exhausted. This will be my first. Sandy is my stepdaughter and I never realized how much a child could get into before this." She sat down when he offered her a seat. "We're here visiting some friends, and so far, Sandy has managed to bring home a puppy and a snake, as well as too many bugs for me to even think about. But I've never seen her so happy."

Gabe noticed that her ankles were swollen, her face and hands a little as well. He put out his hand and she put hers into his, then he rubbed her wrist. She was going to be in a lot of trouble if she didn't keep herself healthy. As casually as he could, he asked her some questions.

"Are you sleeping well? Getting enough to drink?" She said she thought she was, and he nodded, standing up to find his scope, as well a glass of water for her. "May I?"

"Is there something wrong?" He told her that he didn't think so, but it was his habit to make sure that pregnant animals and women were all right. "I've been overdoing it, I know that. When we first got here, the family that we're staying with was nice, but I think we've about overstayed our welcome. There is some hostility going on that wasn't there before. And I have no idea why I just told you that."

"You needed to vent, I would guess." He had her sit up on the examining table after moving the mom and her kittens. "You have anyone here? A doctor, I mean?"

"Am I all right? Do I need to go home now? Jacob is

15

looking for a job. Not having much in the way of luck, but he's been looking." He nodded and listened to the baby. "Please say something." He looked at her and decided to just tell her the truth.

"All right. You need to rest more. Put your feet up and sit back more than you are now. Have someone wait on you for a change, and you need to drink more fluids, not just water." She started to cry. Holding her close to him, he continued. "You're retaining water, and that is not a good thing. You're exhausted, as you admitted to doing too much. And has your doctor told you that you're having twins?"

Goldie looked up at him, shock written all over her face. "I've only seen the clinic doctor at home. And all he told me was that I'm pregnant. Not the friendly type, or else he's bunched me in with the rest of the people he sees. I'm not saying that the others there are dumb and he needs to talk to them like that, but he basically told me that he's too busy to bring more little welfare brats into the world. Plus, he never gave me the feeling that he wanted me to ask questions. In and out was the way things were working there. He's a jerk."

"I understand that. I used to have a practice with a group of people that did the same thing. The more patients you see, the more money you can make." He told her to wait a moment. Going into the hall, he tried to think what he had to do now. His mom came around the corner just as he was reaching for the phone. "Mom, I need your help. I need to set up an appointment for Goldie. Where is her daughter?"

"Your dad took her home with him. He and Caleb's boys are going to play on the swing. They finished putting it up this morning." He nodded. "Tell me what to do and I'll do it."

"I need to get her in for some tests." Gabe told her what

he needed done, then he told her what to say when she called it in. "I want her to have a bed too. Just to keep an eye on her overnight, to make sure that she and the babies are doing all right."

When she walked away, he went back into the room. Goldie was crying, but she did look like she was a little relieved about things. He told her what he wanted her to do. She was shaking her head before he finished.

"I don't have the money for that." He nodded and said it was all right. The hospital would cover it. "No, they won't. They might say that, but in a few days I'll be hit with a huge bill, and we don't have any income right now. Getting here took everything we had, and even things we didn't."

"Let me worry about all that. You, however, need to go in, take a load off your feet, and let me take care of you. If you are indeed carrying twins, things aren't going to be getting better until we get you healthy." She nodded and asked to use his cell phone to call her husband. "Of course, and tell him to bring in a resume. I know for a fact that my brother and sister-in-law are hiring right now."

It took some doing, but he finally convinced her she'd be fine. After he got her settled, he asked Quinn to come by and give him a hand. She said she was on her way now that his dad was going to keep an eye on the kids.

~~~

Jacob wasn't sure what was going on, but he knew that his wife needed medical help. Holding Goldie's hand, he tried to keep up with Dr. Winchester, but he was talking too fast. Finally, he had to put his hand up.

"I'm deaf." Even after all this time, it was hard for him to admit to that. It had been five years, he should be over it by

17

now, he told himself. But Goldie needed him and he couldn't understand the doctor. "Could you speak slower?"

"Yes." The man smiled at him then put out his hand. Without thinking, he touched his fingers to the man's and watched his face. "I'm not human. I know that you're aware of my kind, so I'm going to tell you that I'm a wolf."

Jacob nodded. The people they were staying with, the Waltons of all things, were something else too. He thought they were tigers, but wasn't sure. He also knew that they were scaring his little girl with whatever they were. He might be handicapped, he thought, but he wasn't stupid. He needed this job to make it so they had their own place. Before, he hoped, his child was born.

"Can I taste your blood? I will only need a small bite to talk to you. But I want you to understand fully what is going on with your wife." Jacob told him that he was scared. "Yes, but if she does what I need her to do, and you as well, we'll all come out of this better. Did you know that you were having twins?"

"Yes, Goldie told me when she messaged me." He thought for a moment about this man having his blood, and knew that it wasn't as simple as he was making it sound. But Goldie and Sandy were his family, and he wanted them to be safe. "Yes, you can take my blood."

It wasn't painful at all. And once he did, he knew that the man was trusting him with this, and Jacob wouldn't tell anyone what they'd done. He knew that the Waltons would somehow know, but he'd not tell them the reason he'd done it. They weren't the people he had thought they were.

Your wife is having some issues. Nothing that we can't take care of since we caught it early, but she needs to rest more and keep her feet up. A healthy meal wouldn't hurt either. He nodded and said that they were trying to find a place to live and him a job. *My sister-in-law, Quinn, she's here to interview you. I'd like to say that you will have a job when you leave here, but I won't do that to Quinn. She has a wonderful heart and won't let you go on like this. But if I tell you that she's already hired you, she'll beat my ass.* When the doctor winked at him, Jacob had to laugh. The man was afraid of his sister-in-law. He told him he'd keep his secret.

"Thank you. I don't know what she wants from me, but I'll do my best at it." He said he didn't either, to be honest, and Jacob laughed. "We're living with this couple and their family. They aren't happy that we can't pay them rent, but we just don't have it. I wasn't sure that it was a good idea in the first place, to live with them, but I lost my job about six months ago, and I didn't get unemployment because the company that I worked for didn't pay into it. It took selling everything that we had to make it this far, and the job that they promised us didn't pan out either. There never was one. They wanted us to pay them rent and be their live-in help."

You just be honest with Quinn and we'll work on getting you employed someplace soon. Jacob let out a long breath. *Now, we're going to keep Goldie here for a couple of days. Just to monitor her blood and the babies. After that, I'm going to make sure that they're all doing just fine. If you have any questions, any at all, you can contact me through this link. Just think of me and I can answer you.*

"Thank you so much." Gabe told him it was his pleasure. Jacob believed him too. "I'll have to get going soon. The bus that I ride stops running out to the place I'm staying at four."

I've had them put Goldie in a bigger room, and there is a spare bed in here for you. Sandy is with Quinn and my brother, Caleb,

19

and their three kids. I think they're planning for her to spend the night. Jacob said he didn't have to do that. *You have no idea how excited the boys are to have someone else to play with. And my parents are having a good time watching over them all. It's like Christmas for them.*

Gabe left them after that, giving him the number for his family in case they wanted to check up on their child. And he told him again that the hospital was being taken care of. He hoped so. Jacob had no idea how he was going to afford twins, much less a huge hospital bill.

Jacob watched his wife sleep. Holding her hand, he looked at the band that he'd put there over two years ago, and thought of all the things that she had given him. And how much he'd taken from her. After they were married things hadn't gone all that well. Nothing had, as a matter of fact.

He'd been injured while in the service. The convoy he'd been in had been under siege, and Jacob had taken one in the chest as well as his head. The prognosis wasn't terrible, but soon after he was sent home his hearing started to fade in his left ear. Then a short six months later, he lost it in both. There was money coming in for that, but it wasn't much, and he had a family to take care of.

His wife of four years at that time had left him when it was apparent he was going to receive more attention than she would when they went out. Cindy had decided that to be married to a cripple—her words, not his—was going to be too much for her, as well as having to raise a kid on her own. Jacob had never understood that part…he had been taking care of Sandy all by himself since she'd been born. Cindy never wanted to be bothered, she told him, with a brat. Good riddance to her, but the divorce had cost him not only a good deal of money, but his pride as well.

Then Goldie had come along. She had been dog watching, and he'd met her in the park a few times when he'd been there with Sandy. He never realized that she was in love with him until a few months after Cindy had left him. Jacob had confessed that he was having a difficult time reading stories to his daughter.

"I'm not sure if I'm screaming at her or talking too low. I think she'd tell me, but I don't know." They both laughed, the first one he'd had in a very long time. After that, not only did their friendship bloom, but they fell in love. And Sandy adored Goldie more than she had her own mother when she'd been around.

And now his beloved wife was ill, with his children. As he sat there, trying to figure out what to do, a woman, an incredibly beautiful one, came into the room with him. When he stood up, she offered him a seat and pulled a chair over to sit near him when a second woman came in. He'd met her in the lobby when he arrived as she was a translator for the deaf.

"You know Wendy?" He nodded when Wendy signed the question to him. "Good. I'm Quinn Winchester. I'm here to offer you a job."

"You don't know me." She handed him several sheets of paper, all about him, Goldie, and even his little girl. "How did you get this?"

"I've got some people in high places that know how to get around the curves of a computer." He wasn't sure if he was supposed to think that was funny or not, so he just nodded. "I own two factories here in town. One of them produces a dog food that is natural and safe for dogs. I've worked very hard on that with my dad, and we have a good product. The other makes the bags we use. Also a few other items that we came up with. Such as cat and small animal things. I work very hard, and I'd expect you to as well. But we won't be interfering with your family time. That's important too. Understand?"

Through the translator, he found out what he was going to be paid, his job, and what he was going to be doing in the meantime with his wife. But he did have questions of his own, and she smiled at him. Jacob had a feeling that he was well and deep over his head, something his commanding officer used to say all the time.

"My wife is very ill and we don't have a place to live yet. Then there is babysitting, as well as finding a school for my daughter. No one will rent to us without me having a job." She told him that he had sitters, that Kelley and Sara Winchester were having a grand time with the kids. "Thank you, but I don't want to impose."

"You're not. And trust me, if they thought that you were, they'd tell you. They're not the beat about the bush sort of people. The housing is taken care of as well. I guess that one of the buildings that we own now has a large apartment over it that is monstrous. I haven't seen it yet, but if you'd like we can go now." He looked at his wife. "Gabe said that she'd sleep for about two more hours. He gave her a light sedative that won't hurt the babies."

Jacob went with her, as did Wendy to help him, but he wasn't sure this was a good idea. Things just didn't work this way. This had all started when his wife went to pick up their child, and in turn, they were given free medical care, a job, and a place to live. He was waiting for the other shoe to drop with every step they took to the apartment. The translator got his attention as they were going down in the elevator.

"You can trust these people. I swear to you, there is not a better group of people than these." He asked her if she was related to them. "No. Six months ago, I was living in a box in the alley behind the warehouse she has. Not only did they find me a place to get myself cleaned up—just that, cleaned up—she gave me a job, money, and food. I've never been treated so nicely, and they only want one thing in return. For you to pay it forward when you can."

He entered the large building that looked like it was being cleaned up. There was construction material all over the place, most of it still in the wrapping from the hardware store. Quinn explained to him that there was some development going on at the local library, and they were temporarily holding things here until they needed them.

The ride up in the elevator was short, but smooth. He noticed things like that now. Movement that he could feel, things he could see and smell. Jacob supposed because he'd had his hearing taken from him that he was going to absorb as much as he could with his other senses.

As soon as the elevator opened, he knew that this place was going to be perfect for his little family.

"There are four bedrooms here, and three and a half baths. I never thought about how many bathrooms that is until just now. Anyway, the kitchen is fully updated, and there is a lovely table with six chairs here that you can have. The master bedroom is furnished as well, but the other three aren't. But I have good news on that too. One of the pack members is having a huge garage sale, and they've got a set of bunkbeds, two baby beds, and some dressers. My husband has gone to get them from her." He told her that she was being too generous. "No, we're being helpful. There's a difference."

23

As he walked around the very large place, he thought of living here with his children and wife. It was nicer than the home they'd lost back home. Wandering into the kitchen, he noticed that there was a brand new microwave, and the refrigerator still had the blue plastic wrap around it. He wondered about the people that he was going to be working for, because he knew as well as he was standing there that he was going to.

"You'll start working when your wife is out of the hospital. I've lined up someone to come here and help around the house. They'll keep an eye on your home as well as your family by cooking meals for you and generally cleaning up. We don't want anything to happen to those little babies." He nodded, overwhelmed by their generosity. "We're going to do just fine, Jacob. You just wait and see. And when the family comes here, I should warn you they're very loud, but loving. Welcome to the Winchester family."

Chapter 2

Gabe was finished for the day, yet he sat in his office, about the only thing that wasn't set up yet, and closed his eyes. There was a great deal going on right now, and he just needed a minute to gather his wits about him. He must have dozed off for a bit because when he opened his eyes there was a stranger sitting in his office with him.

"May I help you?" The man shook his head and said that he was fine, for the moment. "Okay, but how did you get in here? I know the doors were locked."

"You don't think a little thing like a lock would keep someone out that wanted to come in, do you? I'm here on behalf of a friend of mine. He wants to know if you've seen a woman." He told him he'd seen a great many women in his time. "Don't be obtuse. I'm being nice here, and I don't want to have to fuck you up to get the information. Her name is Rayne. Rayne McFarland. Ring any bells?"

"No, and even if it did, I'd not tell you if I'd seen her or not." He asked him why not, and pointed out again that he'd been nice. "I don't think you breaking into my office and being all mysterious is being nice. What do you want with this woman?"

"That is none of your business." Gabe reached for his brothers, all of them. He told them that he was in his office and being threatened. "Tell me what I want to know, and you might live long enough to open your practice for the poor and destitute."

"I'm not alone here. You should know that before you go any further." The man told him he was lying. "No, I don't lie. My family is here."

The stranger took a gun out of his pants and laid it on his lap. He told his family what was going on and that the man was looking for someone named Rayne. He asked them to please hurry.

"Now, as I was saying, a friend of mine is looking for this woman, and he will pay you nicely for any and all information you can give him. Or I can just beat the shit out of you, take the information and the money, and still get what we want. I like the latter better myself, but then, I'm like that." Caleb said he was in the lobby and that Dominic and Tyler were coming in the back way. "Tell me what I want to know, Dr. Winchester, and I'll go about my business."

The door opened to his office, but before the man could move, Carmen, a vampire friend of the family, had him lifted from the floor by his neck. Caleb and his dad came in next, and no one said a word. Gabe had never been so glad to see his family than he was at that very moment.

"Now, as I was saying, I don't know anyone by the name of Rayne. Nor do I lie. What's your name?" Gabe wasn't sure if he couldn't speak or wasn't going to, but a quick hard shake from Carmen had him wetting his pants. "She's not terribly happy with your non-answer, if you ask me."

"You'll pay for this. I came here to get information, and you've fucked with the wrong man." When he was set back down on his feet, Carmen grinned at him. "What the fuck do you feed people around here? Or are you a man, honey?"

Carmen put her hands on his head and he screamed. Gabe was sure that he was being mind raped, and not nicely either. Carmen didn't suffer fools well, and she hated bullies. When she let the man go, he fell into a deep sleep. Or she'd killed him. Either way, he knew she'd gotten all they needed.

"His name is Walter Sprintz, the heavy for a man by the name of Carson McFarland. Sprintz here was sent to find McFarland's daughter who has gone missing. Her name is Rayne McFarland." He asked him why they were looking here. "He's following her trail, and this is the last place he was able to find her face. He has tapped into the facial recognition system, and has followed her this far."

"Why?" Carmen told Caleb that Sprintz didn't know, but was told to find her and to bring her back, and as he was a loyal fuck, that's what he was doing. "Is she a kid? Someone that has a drug problem? Why would they search for her?"

"Don't know, but no, not a kid. A grown woman in her mid-twenties." Carmen stretched her arms over her head and said she had to go home for a bit. "Also, he had no idea what you are. Hasn't any clue that we exist. Also, and I find this particularly funny, he has a crush on his boss. McFarland, he thinks, has no idea of his love, but he has it all the same."

After she left, no one said anything. There was a henchman in his office that had pulled a gun on him. The man smelled of urine, and he didn't know what the fuck they were. Gabe looked at his dad and brother when he spoke.

"Now what do we do with him? Other than threatening you, we really don't have much to hold him on. And does he have a permit for that gun?" He told his dad that he had no idea when the rest of his family came into the room with them. "You find anything around? That car of his, it's been around for a couple of days. Seen it myself when I was in town the other day picking up something for your mom."

"Do you suppose this Rayne, whoever she is, is here now? I have to admit, I thought it was Mrs. James he was talking about when he first spoke of the woman." Caleb asked him how he'd gotten in. "Not sure, really. He told me that locks didn't mean anything to people like him. I'm assuming that he means being a crook."

"Well, if it's all the same to you guys, I'm gonna keep my eyes out for this woman. Too bad that we don't have any idea who she might be. Why don't you check your computer? Could be if she's missing, there might be a report on her or something."

Gabe typed her name into the computer and started a search. What popped up startled him. "She's not a child, as Carmen said, but a very beautiful woman. It says here that she recently graduated from college, and that she is to be…No, make that *was* to be wed on June tenth. There isn't anything else about it, other than to say that she'd gotten ill and the wedding has been postponed." Dad asked where it was supposed to be held. "California, but her family resides around here someplace, at least according to this…in the Columbus area. The husband-to-be, Blaine Kline, is said to be the most eligible bachelor of all time, and he lives around here too. I wonder why California then? Oh well, not my problem."

Dad snorted. "Might be 'eligible' to himself, but if she ran off, I'm thinking that he's not as good as he thinks he might be." Gabe had to agree. "Any pictures?"

He scrolled through the articles about the woman and found a better picture than the one posted from her graduation. This was a picture of her at a wedding where she must have been a bridesmaid. He showed it to his family. He started reading what the caption said.

"Will there be wedding bells in the future for Ms. McFarland? Sources tell us yes, but Ms. McFarland said there wasn't anyone special in her life." He looked at the date on the article. "This was a short month before her wedding announcement. Where, I might add, there is no picture of the bride-to-be."

"Sounds like she's been sold off." Everyone looked at his dad. "Well, think on it. She ain't got no one special in her life. There ain't no dad-burn picture of her in the paper, and now her father is out looking for her. He was forcing her into this thing and she didn't care for it. I'm thinking that if you look up that other fella, you'll see that he's a putz."

So, he did. And what a putz he was. "It says here that Mr. Kline is a college grad with a general degree. Could mean that he barely made it through college or just paid for it." He had no idea why he thought that, but he was having fun. "He lives on the estate of his parents, who are still alive and more than likely footing the bills for some...."

He read the rest of the article with the announcement to himself. When he finished, he couldn't even fathom why this man, Spintz, had come back to haunt them. He was just trying to figure out how to not tell anyone what he'd just figured out when Caleb spoke.

29

"What did you find?" He looked at Caleb, then back at the monitor. "Gabe, what is it? Is he dead? Did she murder him?"

"No, but we might. You know him. Or his family." He asked him how. "Klinegate. Does that ring any bells for you?"

He knew the moment his brother got it. He stood up and looked over his shoulder as he read the rest of the article. It mentioned the trouble that they'd had with him when Caleb had been in college.

"There was a scandal some years ago, at the university that Blaine Kline graduated from. Charges were later dropped by the college when sufficient information wasn't forthcoming." Gabe laughed as he finished the article, trying to make light of the situation. "I'm sure that once Daddy found out about it, he paid to make sure that it wasn't forthcoming. Dad, you had it right, he is a putz."

Caleb looked angry. He'd been embarrassed back then. And they all believed that since they didn't have the finances to pay for a fancy lawyer, he'd lose his degree as well as all the money that their parents had scraped together for them to go to college.

"We all had to take the test again. Each of us in that class was accused of cheating, and if we failed, then they knew who had gotten the answers." Dad asked Caleb how they thought that. "Of the hundred and sixteen in the class, all but four didn't make a perfect score. And since it was all multiple choice, they had no way of seeing if they would have had the same written answers. I think of the second test scores, myself and one other person scored perfectly, and Blaine, Walter, and their buddies didn't even pass it."

"And that didn't tell them that he cheated?" Gabe told

Dad that money talks. "I guess it does. I ever find out you boys do something like that now that we have some money, I'll take you to the wood shed, and there won't be none of that playing around either."

They all answered him in unison. "Yes, sir." Their dad was a good man, seldom angry, but when he needed to take you to the shed, which was only a shed because it had a roof over it, then you knew you were in trouble. Gabe had got his butt walloped only the one time, and that was enough for him.

"I think we should just keep an eye out for this woman, and dump this man back in his car. He'll have a hell of a headache, but he won't stop, I don't think. And I for one do not want him coming around our family again." Gabe asked him why he would think that he wouldn't stop. "Money, as we've discovered, can make people do the strangest things. And until we figure out number one, if she's around, and number two, what made her run, we're going to lay low and let this asshole hang himself. And I have no doubt that if he fucks up, he might just do that. Carmen will help him."

~~~

Rayne watched the men carrying Wally out to his car and dumping him in it. They weren't very nice about it either. That made her laugh, but she quickly covered her mouth so that no one would hear her. Not that there were many people around, but she still didn't want to be caught by her father's men. Things were heating up if her dad's second was here in this town. But she was stuck here, for now anyway.

The car that she'd been driving had broken down about three miles out of town. And no matter what she did, it wouldn't run. Rayne knew how to work on them and a great

31

many other things, but the car had died and she'd given it a nice sendoff by shoving it into a cave about half a mile from where she'd been stranded. She hated to do that, but she had a madman on her tail and she didn't want him to catch her. Not now, not ever. Her dad was nuts.

He'd told her when she came home from her cousin's wedding that it was about time she got married too. Rayne had been living on her own since graduating from high school, and had put herself through college by working odd jobs and waiting tables. Dad showing up at her apartment and letting himself in had not only pissed her off, but scared her a little. Dad had been ignoring her for years now, and this little visit wasn't how he usually got messages to her. Wally was the one that would bring them around, and his fists too. Compliments of dear old Dad, he told her.

"No thanks. I don't want to marry yet. I have things I want to do." He had tossed a newspaper in front of her. It not only said she was getting married soon, but to one of his business partners. "I'm not marrying Blaine. He's about your age."

"Not him, his son, Blaine Junior. And you will, Rayne. I need this deal to go through, and you're the bait at the end of the hook." She didn't bother telling him she was twenty-six years old and usually made her own decisions. "You'll marry in June. It'll be a big wedding that you'll let a staff deal with. I don't want you fucking it up by wanting it your way. And you'll come home. I want the world to know that you and I are the best of friends. After that, I'll buy you a lovely home, and you can have as much money as you want to furnish it. I'll even spring for a honeymoon in Europe if you want."

"What I want seems to be irrelevant, don't you think? It seems you have it all taken care of. Do you have my ovulation schedule? Do you have a baby planned out too?" The punch to her face knocked her back into the wall, but she got up quickly. "Big man. Hitting the person you need something from."

"Wipe your mouth off and shut up. The wedding will go on, Rayne, or so help me, you'll not marry because you'll be dead." Rayne hadn't looked in the direction of the camera that she had going in this room as well as the others she lived in. "Now, here is the way it's going to go. You'll marry Blaine, and after a time, I'll allow you to have a lover. I don't want you to have a child with any of them, so you'll have that taken care of before you marry. No children, do you hear me? And if you don't want to do that, I can have Walter come here and beat you enough that you can't have one without killing yourself. I'd rather do it the easy way, but that's entirely up to you."

She didn't say another word to him after that. In her head, she was plotting and planning, glad now that she'd been smart enough to get things ready to go when she'd moved out. Her dad was a criminal, and she had taken what she could from him to get as far from him and his kind as possible if he ever got it in his head to use her. Now her life sat in a duffle bag, just waiting for her to pick up and go. Rayne had left the next afternoon when she'd gone to work and slipped out the back in a delivery truck.

That had been five months ago. Thankfully, with help, she'd been about a half step ahead of the men he'd sent for her since. Twice she had seen Wally before he saw her, and that had her running again. Coming here, to this little town, had been an emergency, and she'd been here three weeks and thought she was safe. Now, here was Wally again. Rayne turned from the window to see a little girl staring at her.

"Hello." She sat down on the floor, not wanting to startle her. Rayne knew enough to know that the child would frighten easily and not have any idea what she was doing. "Can I help you?"

"I don't know. Where am I?" She looked around, but Rayne watched her. "How did I get here?"

"My name is Rayne." The girl looked at her. "When I was born, my mom told me that it was raining very hard, hard enough that my dad's plane was delayed by two days. So, that's why she named me that. To give me good luck."

She just stared at her, not saying anything, just looking confused. Rayne told her about her childhood, how she'd grown up in a cold house with no love. The little girl glanced around again and then frowned.

"I was running, and then I found myself here." Rayne asked her why she was running. "He was chasing me."

"All right. I want you to close your eyes and tell me where you are right now." The girl looked around then back at her. "You're not here. You are aware of that much, aren't you?"

"Yes, I came because they told me to." Rayne told her that many people like her knew her. "I know. They told me that you'd be able to help me go home."

"I will. Close your eyes and tell me what you see. Why are you running?" She reached out and put her hand on the child's. She was cold, her fingers like small shards of ice.

"It's dark outside."

She could have told the little girl what she saw, could have helped her through this, but didn't. Rayne knew that she'd have to do this on her own or there would be no peace for her. As she watched her remember, Rayne saw the trees start to form, and their color told her it was early fall. Perhaps only a year ago.

"My sister and I were playing in the yard. Momma was...I don't know. I can't see her." Rayne asked after her sister. "She's...I can't find her either. We never go anywhere without each other. Do you think she's all right?"

"It's all right. Just one thing at a time. What's your name? Do you remember?" The child sat down...remembering took its toll on her. "My name is Rayne. My mom named me that when I was born. It was raining and she said it would be good luck."

"Where am I?" Rayne repeated everything to her once again. Eventually she'd remember, but only in bits and pieces. "I was running from my stepdad."

"What did he want from you?" She frowned again. "Tell me about your sister. Can you see her yet?"

"We were in the woods, behind our house. It was pretty out...Mom said it was going to be cold soon, and we should enjoy the weather." Rayne waited. "He hated us. And he said we were...Mom told me to run. To get away. He had hit her again."

"All right. You're doing very well. I forgot your name." The little girl looked at her. "Mine is Rayne. When I was born—"

"April. My sister is Rose." Rayne nodded and smiled. "He killed me, didn't he? That's why I don't know where I am."

"Yes, how did he kill you, April? Did he kill Rose too?" She nodded. "I'm so sorry about that. Did your mom help him?"

"Yes, she didn't want to. Mom tried to protect us. I think she's dead too." Rayne asked her where she was. April had it now, knew all that there was to remember about her murder. "It's cold and I...Rose is with me. We're...we're in the well at the back of my house. It's deep. Will you help me?"

"Yes, I will. I need just a few more things from you to make the police go and find you." She nodded and looked around again. Rayne thought she was slipping again, but she told her that she was so sad. "I am as well. You are too young, both of you, to have been killed like this."

"He said that I was a drain to him. I don't know what that meant so I asked him." Rayne told her she was sorry again. "His name. You need it. His name is Richard Fox. My mom called him Dick."

She remembered the name in the papers a few months back. How he had taken the money from the fund that had been set up to help find the girls. Rayne couldn't remember if the mother was missing at that time, but knew that she had recently disappeared herself. The strain of her daughters being gone had driven her to commit suicide, everyone thought, but now she knew. He had killed her too when she wanted to bring her babies home to be buried.

April sat there for several more minutes, and Rayne let her. Pulling her bag to her, she got one of the burner phones that had no attachment to her whatsoever, and put in the little device to hide where she was.

"Are you going to help me?" Rayne told her that she was doing it right now. "I should go then. To wait. Rose, she can't come out. Or, I think she doesn't want to."

"I'm sorry, April." She heard the clicking of her phone and then the connection. "April and Rose Delaney are in the well under a newly poured concrete foundation at the back of the property where they lived. Stepfather Richard Fox, aka Dick Fox, killed them both. The murder weapon is with them."

Closing the connection, she waited one minute. And when the return call came in, she took off the device then destroyed the phone and took out the SIM card. She looked at April, and could see now the damage that had been put upon her at death.

"You knew, didn't you?" Rayne told her that she had when she touched her. "They told me, when I was wandering around, that I had to find you. And that though you don't ever ask for something in return, that I could help you too."

"Some do, but it's not necessary." April nodded. "You can go in peace now. The man that I called, he and I have a relationship, and he knows when I call and give him what I know, he'll be able to close a case. I've never met him, but he can be trusted to find you."

"There is a man that is hunting for you, your father." She told her that she knew that. "A family is here, one that you can trust over anyone else. Their name is like the gun. I can't remember it. Things are...I think things are fading for me."

"They will. When you are found, which I think will be soon, you must move on. You have no reason to stay around. The longer you are here, the more will fade from you until you are nothing but a shadow of yourself. You must move on." April said that she would. "I'm glad that you found me, April, and I'm glad that I could help."

"Find the gun family." She said that she would if she needed them. "You will. Sooner than you think. Find them, and be safe for more like me."

When April left her, Rayne laid down. It didn't exhaust her to help the dead, but it hurt her in ways that she could never explain. And when it was children who suffered, she was in a great deal of pain. Not that she talked about it anymore. People were weirded out when they found out she could talk to the dead. Most didn't believe her, but those that did, they wanted her to talk to them to get information. Much like her dad did. And, she supposed, Blaine.

Chapter 3

Owen walked up and down the grocery aisles. He didn't know what he wanted for dinner, and was waiting for something to pop out and inspire him. So far, the only thing that had inspired him was the new employee that was currently stocking the cereal shelf. He passed by her again, on the pretense of looking at the sugary treats. Not that he indulged in them, but he would to get her name and number. Owen paused and looked behind him, calling on his wolf to help him sniff the air to see if he knew the man that was speaking.

"Do you know this woman?" The man's voice was cultured, his accent was slight, but he'd say southern for sure. As he rounded the next endcap, he looked for the source. "She's been kidnapped and we're looking for her."

"Nope, haven't seen her."

He moved on and Owen followed as the man went from person to person, asking the same thing of each of the dozen or so people in the store. Finally, he got to him.

"You seen this woman?" Like the others, he looked at the picture and said that he'd not. "She's been taken against her will, and we think she might have gotten away."

"No. I'm sorry. I've not seen her. How do you know that she might have gotten away? I mean, if she'd been taken against her will, how would any of us have seen her?" He stared at him for several seconds and Owen stared right back, letting a little of his wolf go in case the man got the wrong idea about him. That he was a pushover.

Meanness felt like it dripped from the man. Like he was so hard and harsh that he couldn't contain it. As he stood there, shifting a little, Owen saw the gun, like he was sure he'd been meant to.

"You're asking a lot of questions for someone that hasn't seen her." Owen said it was only the one. "Still, none of your fucking business what we think about her getting away. Did you see her or not?"

"Nope." He started away when his arm was grabbed. Owen put his hand over the man's and let his paw surface. "Let me go or lose your hand. I'm not one to fuck with, buddy."

The man cried out when Owen dug deeper with his claws, and when he jerked away from him, blood pouring from the fresh wound, Owen sniffed it before licking some of it from his hand. The stranger backed away, but it was too late now. He not only had his scent, but a part of him that would mean his death should he fuck up.

Owen reached out to his family and let them all know what he'd found. Just before he decided that he'd like a pizza for dinner with them, a woman came out from the back of the store and stared at him. Owen shook his head ever so slightly and then looked away. He could not believe that the very woman in the picture was right here.

Making sure the man left the place, slowly, so as not to scare her, he made his way to the doors that led to the butcher area. He wasn't sure that she'd still be there, but when he slipped behind the swinging doors, Rayne was still there. And she looked like she was hurt. Then he could smell the blood.

"Did he find you?" She shook her head then nodded. "Okay, that wasn't terribly helpful. Do you know who the man is? The one that was there with me?"

"Yes, he's one of my dad's henchmen. You tossed Wally, Ben's boss, out on his ass the other day. Probably when he was looking for me." Owen told her how he'd threatened his brother. "Figures. I was told to find you. I had to figure out what it meant, that I was to look for the gun family, but Winchester, that was stumping me."

"You need medical help." She nodded and leaned heavily against the counter. He thought that he'd figure out later what she meant by the gun comment, but right now he needed to get her to someone that could keep her identity safe, and her as well. "I have a brother that is a doctor. We can take you there."

"We?" He said that Xander, another brother, was coming to help him. "I fell in the woods. I was helping...well, I wasn't helping so much as I was trying to make sure that something was done for me. I fell in a hole and stabbed myself on a piece of wood."

When she lifted her shirt up, he saw the bloodstained towel that she had tied around her. Stepping closer to her in the event that she fell, Owen told his brother what was going on. Pulling away the towel, he stared at the wound, then grabbed her up when she simply slumped forward. She looked up at him when he said her name.

"I can't go back to him. He'll kill me." He said she wasn't going anywhere. "Please, don't tell him. He'll kill you all should he find me with you. Protect me, please."

"I will." Xander came to the back where they were and simply asked him what he needed. "I have to get out of here with no one seeing her. And there is a guy that is looking for her."

Carmen came in the room with them. She was just suddenly there. When she took the woman from him and disappeared, telling them that she was headed to Gabe, he looked at Xander.

"A man was here. He was asking about her and I looked up and there she was." Xander asked if the blood on his hand was hers or his. "The man's. She said his name was Ben, nothing more."

Taking his hand to his mouth, Xander licked some of the blood. He told him, just in case, to not wash up until he saw the rest of them. As they made their way to the front of the store, he could see droplets of blood from the man. When they disappeared at a parking space that was now empty, he knew that he was going to find him and see what else he knew.

"What did she say to you?" He told him what she'd said. "What do you suppose she meant by the gun? I mean, yeah, there are Winchester rifles, but there had to be more than that."

"I was more concerned with her bleeding out than I was playing twenty questions with her." Xander just cocked a brow at him. "I'm sorry. It's been a hell of a day, and that man, he just felt bad. Like evil in a way that I've never encountered before."

They were nearly to the office when he realized that Carmen was standing outside the building. He pounded on the door, and when he got no answer, he called out to his brother. Gabe said he was on his way from the hospital and would be there soon. They let themselves in and put the woman on the table to be examined. Owen hoped that he had done the right thing with Rayne. There was just something so calming about her.

When she woke a couple minutes after Xander left, he got up to take her hand into his. She was in pain, a great deal of it, but she was fighting through it to talk to him. On the second try to get her mouth moving, she spoke quietly and quickly.

"My father, you know who he is, correct?" He said only what he had seen in the paper. "He's worse, ten times ten times...you get the picture. If he figures out that you're harboring me, he's going to kill us all. I don't want that to happen. Get the doctor to patch me up, and I'll leave."

"Owen?" He turned to look at Gabe when he said his name a second time. "Step away from her, Owen. I don't want to hurt you."

"She's already hurt." He saw him then, his brother's wolf sliding along his skin, and he wasn't happy. As he stood in front of Rayne to protect her, Gabe growled low and told him to step away from his mate. "Christ, are you kidding me? Now? You're finding your mate now? With this woman? Will this madness never stop?"

"What the fuck is wrong with you?" He looked at Rayne when she spoke. "Just patch me up and I'll leave before my father comes looking. And you don't want that to happen."

"Yeah, well, that just went down shit creek with all the

paddles." She stared at him, then closed her eyes. Owen looked at Gabe as he moved to the other side of the room. "Mom and Dad are going to have a cow...you know that, don't you? And then they're going to be harping on—"

"Owen, shut up." He snapped his mouth closed quickly. Gabe moved to the table, but he didn't touch her. "She's been hurt, do you know how?"

Owen told him everything that he knew. "I'm sorry for freaking out just now. I mean, there has been some major shit going down lately, and now you have a mate."

"Yes, I do. I'm going to have to put her out so I can look at her wound. Would you stay?" He asked if he was going to hurt him if he did. "No. I believe we're under control now. I think he could smell who she was before I did, and knew she was hurt. Probably thought that you'd done it. I don't know."

"I'll help you. While I tell you what I know, which isn't much. Oh, and Dad and Mom, they both know that we've brought her here. I called for backup and everyone answered it." Gabe said that was all right while he cut away her blouse. "She said that she was in the woods checking up on something. What do you suppose it was?"

"Speaking of woods. Did you hear that they found those little girls?" He said that he hadn't. "That's where I was, making arrangements to do an autopsy on them. They were in the well at the back of their home in plastic bags. The murder weapon is intact too. They're running the prints, but I think we both know who murdered them."

Their stepfather had been the one. The entire family had thought that from the beginning, but without the bodies or a witness, he'd been set free. However, he knew that everyone was keeping an eye on him. Then just a few months ago, his wife had committed suicide and hadn't left a note. She had been depressed, even going so far as to cut her wrists once. Nothing could bring her out of it...she said she missed her little girls.

Helping Gabe, Owen wondered what his brother would do now. It was obvious that she was on the run...they had been accosted by men looking for her for days now. So, what made her dad want her so badly that he'd send someone to bring her home? What did she know about him that made him so nervous?

~~~

Gabe cleaned up after he'd done all he could do for his mate. It had hurt his wolf to know that she was in pain. After he'd cleaned up the wounds he went ahead and sealed the wounds as his wolf. He knew she'd be fine, but he did worry about her. She kept calling for someone by the name of Anna.

Opening his computer up, he looked up the family again. This time he paid attention to names, and found out that her mom was Anna. He wondered why she was calling her by her given name rather than Mom, but wouldn't be able to ask until she woke. As he was getting ready to lie down on the little cot in his office, he checked on her once more. He was surprised to find her not just awake, but trying to stand as well.

"Don't. You'll start bleeding again." She wouldn't, but it had the desired effect. "You're going to be all right, but I want you to be still for a few more days. You could get an infection."

She laid down, but she didn't look happy. "Look, don't lie to me. I know that you're not human and that you fixed the wounds as your wolf. I'm weak, but not stupid. Don't treat

45

me that way." He laughed. "What is so funny?"

"I have no idea, but you seem to know a great deal about what I did to you for someone that was out. You have an insider? Cameras in my office?" She looked to his left and he did as well. "Are you hungry?"

"Yes." She looked to his left again and so did he. "You're my mate. You're…I'm not sure what that entails, but I'm going to be safe with you. You're a Winchester."

"I am." He looked again before sitting on the chair by her bed. "I'm not sure what's going on, but yes, I'm your mate and a Winchester. Owen said that you talked about a gun and it tripped you up."

"I'm supposed to tell you everything. I'm not sure that's a good idea, but since she's never steered me wrong before, I suppose I'll have to trust her judgment on this one too. Do you believe in the hereafter?" He said that he wasn't sure what she meant. "You know, ghosts and dead people. They're here, all the time. You have one in your office right now. He has been hanging around here for decades, and is glad to have the company."

He looked to his left and she told him on the right. Staring at the wall, the blank wall, he wasn't sure what to say to her. Ghosts? Dead people? Gabe asked her if she'd bumped her head.

"Several times, but that's not what made it so I can see ghosts. I was strangled with the cord as a baby. No fault of anyone's, but just something that happens. My mother told me that they took nearly five minutes to revive me." Gabe asked her who she was looking at. "Right now? Mr. Calm is on your right, and my mom, Anna, is on your left. She is the one that told me to find you, after April did."

46

"April, the little girl that was found today?" Rayne nodded. "I'm confused. From what I saw of the body earlier, she's been dead for a long time. Perhaps as long as she's been missing."

"Yes, a year. She came to me this morning, and I called a friend of mine and he found her. Her and her sister, Rose. April told me where she was and who did it. I knew, of course, but she had to figure it out." He stood up and moved away from her. "Am I freaking you out?"

"Yes, a great deal. No one, not even the staff at the hospital, knows that there were two bodies in that well. How did you...are those the woods that you fell in? You were there?" She told him she'd been making sure that April was finally at peace. "I don't understand."

"I know, and I'm sorry." She sat up, and he steadied her a little as she started talking again. "My name is Rayne McFarland. I can speak to and see ghosts. My mom, since she was killed, has been helping me out. She can...I guess she's been the one that has trained me for this job."

"It's a job for you." Gabe was pacing now. He wasn't sure, but he thought his mate was off her rocker. "I don't know, how much does it pay? Or do you and your mom split the costs?"

"You're an asshole." He nodded, too distracted to tell her he was usually a nice guy. "My mom said to tell you that you have twenty-seven cents and a movie ticket stub in your pocket, and seventy-four dollars in your wallet."

Gabe pulled the change out of his pocket and laid it on the table near the bed she was in. He counted it three times before he looked at her. There was twenty-seven cents, as well as the stub to the movie he'd seen last night. Gabe sat down on the chair again.

"You can see ghosts." Rayne nodded. "All right. I'm not saying that I'm completely convinced, but let's say that you do. What does your father want from you then? Does he have a ghost that he needs to talk to?"

"Yes." He waited for more, and he wasn't sure she was going to tell him. "Several months ago, before I left, he had a partner. Jamie wasn't a nice man, but he wasn't nearly as bad as my dad is. Anyway, Jamie was killed in an automobile accident. Which, I guess you could say wasn't such a bad thing, but he had taken a great deal of money from Daddy dearest just that afternoon. The accident was just that, an accident, but Dad was a suspect in his death."

"He was arrested and detained for several weeks." He'd read about it in the papers while doing a search after he'd been visited by Sprintz. "I think they let him go, with the understanding that he was going to be watched."

"Yes, well, that never works out for them. He's slick and has too many people working for him that cover for him nicely." Gabe nodded and asked her what this had to do with her. "Nothing, not really, but my dad got it in his head that I could use my freakiness and find the money for him. I told him where he could shove it and let it go. I thought he had as well, until he came to visit me at my home. You have to understand that up until that moment, I didn't think he believed me when I told him who I could talk to. I think, in this, he's trying to hedge his bets and get his money returned."

"So, you ran." Rayne told him that she did, but not for that. "Your father, if you don't mind me saying so, isn't a nice guy."

"No shit. I was at my cousin's wedding. It was a nice

affair, and I came home a few days after it. When I got home my dad was there, waiting for me. He told me that it was time I got married." Gabe asked if it was Blaine Kline. "Yes, you're very well informed. When I told him that I wasn't marrying Plain Blaine, he told me that he was going to knock some sense into me. Blaine, not my dad. Even though my dad hit me that day, he said that Blaine was going to make me do as I was told when I was told. He has methods. I left a few days later, and have been on the run ever since."

Gabe got up to pace again. He had so many thoughts going through his head right now that he wasn't sure he could have put any of them into questions. Like, how did she make it to here? To him? How did she know about the children in the well? He wasn't ready to believe the ghosts thing yet, but he had no other answers.

"My brothers know Blaine. I've never heard him called Plain Blaine, but from what I understand, it suits him. Blaine was caught up in a cheating scandal when my brother Caleb was in college. It was never proven, and a few months after it started Blaine graduated from college, and nothing more was said about it." She asked if his brother had cheated. "No, not Caleb. He's smart and ambitious, but he'd never do that."

"So, you still don't believe me?" He stopped pacing and looked at her. "I know it's a lot to take in, but Anna said that you need to know now so that when the time comes for me to help someone, you won't freak out."

"You think I will." Rayne shrugged and looked to her right. "Is there someone here now? Someone that wants you to help them?"

"Yes, Anna wants to know why you don't think I'm telling you the truth when it's known that I can't lie to you?"

He told her if she believed it then it wasn't a lie as far as she was concerned, thus she thought she was not lying. "Okay, I can buy that, but this man, he needs me. If you would just sit quietly, I think I can prove something to you."

"I don't think you should leave here." Rayne said that she wasn't, but got up to sit on the floor. He sat down next to her when she told him to. "What do I need to do?"

"Just be very quiet and don't do anything stupid." Gabe said he wasn't known for doing stupid things. "Well, maybe not under normal circumstances, but this isn't normal for you. Seeing the dead, I mean."

Before he could ask her what that meant, she grabbed his hand. He curled his fingers into hers, liking the feel of it, when something moved in front of him. He wasn't sure what to think, so he concentrated hard on the image that was coming clearer with each passing minute. Rayne was speaking quietly and slowly, repeating herself several times when he saw him.

His first instinct was to jerk back from her, but she held his hand tighter. And when the man, someone that he thought looked familiar, glanced at him, he was as shocked as he'd ever been. He started to ask him where he'd been all these years when Rayne told him to be still.

"Do you know where you are?" Mr. Bishop turned away from him to look at Rayne while she spoke to him. "Can you tell me why you came to me?"

"They said you could help me. I know him." Gabe nodded when he asked him. "I know it. Your name is…Where am I?"

"You have to tell me. You know, just close your eyes and think." Mr. Bishop did as he was told, but kept opening one eye to look at him. "He's going to help me. Do you know him?"

"Gabriel. Gabriel Winchester. I heard you were back in town." Gabe nodded. "You were in my science class. Dated my...my daughter. I have a daughter."

"Yes, you do. Do you know her name?" He had no idea why he was doing this, but he knew that he couldn't just blurt out information. "Where are you?"

"Samuel Bishop. I was a science teacher at the high school." Gabe nodded at him. "I don't know how I got here. I was...I went to bed and then I was here. Where is my daughter?"

"Who is she?" Mr. Bishop shook his head. "You know her, don't you? You have a daughter. What is her name?"

"Beth. Elizabeth Bishop. She had leukemia and you took her to her prom." Gabe said that he had. "Nicest thing you could have done for her. She died three days later, just as peaceful as...I'm dead too. I had a heart attack and died."

"Yes, I'm sorry." He nodded. Gabe looked at Rayne. Now that the man remembered—he supposed that was what he'd come here for—Gabe had no idea of what to do now. Rayne was staring at him, then looked at Mr. Bishop. "I can go now, can't I? I was looking for someone, and now I know I can move on."

"She's here to take you." They both looked behind Mr. Bishop. Gabe couldn't see anyone, but apparently, Rayne and Mr. Bishop could. "You go with her now. And talk. It's what you needed."

Gabe sat there not moving, nor asking any questions. There were plenty of them to ask, but he couldn't nail a single one of them down well enough to form it. He looked over at Rayne when she said his name. Shaking his head, he asked her to wait.

"We have to go. Anna said that he's coming."

51

He stood up and made his way to the door. She nodded when he asked if they could go out the back door, and he slipped out the back and into his truck with her right beside him. They were nearly to his home when he realized what had just happened. He'd talked to the dead.

Chapter 4

Blaine looked out the window of his hotel. He loved
big cities, and Columbus was one of the nicest he'd been
in looking for his errant wife-to-be. Rayne had caused him
enough shit to last several lifetimes. And when he got her,
because there wasn't any doubt that he would, he was going
to make her pay for each and every piece of shit place he'd
had to stay in. The looks he'd gotten from people when she'd
left him high and dry with his dick in his hand, as well as the
time and energy spent on hunting her down, was going to be
her worst nightmare.

"Sir, we can't seem to locate Mr. Sprintz." He turned and
looked at Jim, his secretary. "We have someone going to the
hospital now, but we don't have any way of knowing what
name he might be using, so it will be tricky."

"Check the morgue. That is where he'd better be if he
doesn't find Rayne soon." The man left him and he turned to
look out the window again. "Where the fuck are you, Rayne?"

When he'd been told that he was going to marry the girl,

he'd balked. Then he'd been set down with a meeting between him, his dad, and Mr. McFarland. It was both enlightening as well as funny that the man had told him about the ghosts.

"My daughter is a freak. She sees and talks to ghosts, apparently. Claims to see my dead wife too." Blaine asked if he was joking. "No, not at all. I mean, I surely don't believe her, but she does and that's what matters. Everywhere she goes, she speaks to them. Like they're her best friends or something. She moved out of the house when I forbade her to bring it up again. Christ, it was a nightmare. But now, I have a use for it, if she's telling the truth. But she won't do what I tell her. Not even the threat of taking her out of the will has done a damned thing to make her see it my way."

"Then why the hell would you think I'd want to marry her? I have no desire to have a fucking nutball in my life." Carson nodded and smiled. "I don't think I can do this. Not worth my time for a little pussy occasionally."

"She's a looker, but that's not all. I'll settle with you. Ten million as soon as you say I do and sleep with her. I'll fork over another five million every year after that. Then if you give me a grandson—and I do mean you give the little fucker to me—I'll hand over fifty million. So long as it's hers and yours and nobody else's that you might fuck along the way. I told her that I didn't want any brats from her, but a grandson, given to me, means I can mold him into what I want, not some pussy assed kid that takes after her." Blaine asked him why that was important that she marry at all. "I need someone to keep her in line, make her do what I want and to make sure that she doesn't go around talking to the dead. Unless it's someone I need her to talk to. You can do that, can't you? Keep your wife in line?"

54

"Yes, if you've read anything about me, you know that I can, and do have my idea of fun. But you'd subject your daughter to this? Without a care in the world?" Carson said he'd put it in writing if he wanted him to. "All right. I'll do it. I don't believe she actually talks to them, do you?"

"No, Christ no, but if she can, I want to control it." He asked him again why. "I have me a dead business partner that took my money and I can't find it. If I can get it from wherever he stashed it, I'll give you a percentage of that too. Fair enough?"

"Yes."

But even after he'd signed all the paperwork and gotten a little advance on the money for the wedding, he still didn't believe that she could see anything at all and was dicking with her father. But she never would him. He'd knock that shit out of her right from the start.

"Ghosts. Like who the fuck believes in that shit?" He sat down and took another sip of his whiskey. A poor man's drink, to be sure, but he enjoyed it more than he did the crap that his dad drank. Who the fuck liked sherry?

He thought about the conversation, what he'd been told about Rayne, and the pictures of her they'd shown him. Not bad, he'd thought, but pictures could be played with. But a couple of weeks after that, he'd seen her. Christ, who would have thought that a crazy woman could look like every man's jerkoff fantasy? And he had used those images even when he'd been fucking a hooker.

The knock at his door came at the same time his cell was going off. He had to take both, so he went to the door and opened it as he answered the phone. He was told a couple of days ago, that he was never to ignore calls from Carson

McFarland again. It had been a very painful lesson.

There wasn't anyone at the door, so he started to close it when he saw him. He didn't know him, and had no idea why he was at his door. Just as Blaine was about to close the door again, the man stepped into his room and nodded at the chair. It was the gun that had him going to sit.

"Are you listening to me?" He had forgotten about the phone call, and told Carson that he had a visitor. "What sort of visitor? Are you bringing fucking whores to your room? You mother fucker, you're supposed to be waiting on your wife."

The gun at his head had him swallowing twice. "It was the wrong room. I'm not bringing whores to my room." The gun moved away from his head, but it was still out. "Have you heard anything about Rayne? And so you know, Sprintz is missing."

"I've got a man on that." The man in the room with him sat down but didn't speak. "When you find her, you're going to teach her what it means to fuck with me and you, aren't you?"

"Yes." He eyed the man in front of him. For some reason, Blaine had it in his head that he could hear every word that was being said. "I should be leaving here in the next few hours."

The man with the gun shook his head and smiled. Blaine had to admit he was a little afraid of the man and any reason why he might be there. After a few more minutes of small talk and threats to Rayne, he closed his cell.

"What the fuck are you doing in here?" The man reached into his jacket pocket and showed him his badge. "So? I'm here looking for my future wife. There isn't anything the Feds need to be coming here and harassing me about."

"Isn't there? Not the way I see it. We found her, by the way." He asked him where Rayne was. "Not Ms. McFarland, but Sherry Contrail."

"Am I supposed to know who that is?" He handed him a picture and Blaine knew. "Again, am I supposed to know who this Contrail person is? And why would I even care?"

"You murdered her. We know that you did because you were sloppy. And your MO was all over this one. Just like Jeri Shipley and Grace Davenport." Blaine had worked hard on his poker face. He knew for a fact there would be no tells on his person that would make this man think he was making him squirm, even just a little. "No? Well, how about Ms. McFarland? You planning to do to her what you did to the others?"

"Since I have no idea what you're talking about, I would remind you that she is my future wife, and I won't tolerate you saying anything bad about her." The man stared at him for several seconds before he threw back his head and laughed. "And you find this funny, why?"

"You, you think to throw me off the scent, when I know for a fact that inside your slimy skin you're oozing sweat. I've always wondered when I come across sick fucks like your kind what makes you think that anyone else likes cleaning up your messes. Just a query. One that I don't suppose you're going to answer for me, are you?" Blaine sat very still, his body inside just as the man described it. "I have a deal for you, Kline. One that, in your position, you should take. It's about your future wife and her daddy. You see, we know the plan that you have with him. The way that you've been given...let's call it carte blanche to do as you wish to the girl. Your way of doing this,

57

you end up with poison running through your system when you're caught. My way, should you chose to take it, is for you to spend the rest of your natural life behind bars."

"Even if I were to think of this deal, neither one of them holds much in the way of perks for me." He told him that he wasn't dead and that had to be a perk. "To you, I suppose it would be. But behind bars? I don't think so. I have a good life on the outside of prison, and I plan to keep it that way."

"Suit yourself." The man stood up. "Oh, before I forget to tell you. We've made sure that McFarland knows about our little meeting. We don't want him to think that his choice for his son-in-law is without its own set of issues."

Blaine didn't move. Not when he left him, nor when his cell phone started to ring again. This Fed—and he surely wished that he'd been able to read his name—was going to ruin a lot of things for him, and cause his untimely death if he couldn't convince Carson that he'd not said a single word to him about the deal or what was planned. Then there were the deaths of the women. Christ, what sort of sloppy was he talking about?

He'd worn a condom when fucking them. Blaine was naked when he killed them, assuring himself that no blood or shoe patterns could be found. He'd made sure that he washed them up well when he was finished creating his bloodbath with his victims. There wasn't any way, none whatsoever, that he left anything of himself behind, nor did he have a signature. He made sure that he had no MO when he was having his fun, except that he killed them.

The more Blaine thought about it, he thought of what the Fed had said. Did cleaning up after himself count as an MO? Surely not. He knew guys that killed the same way every time they did it. The same gun, the same kind of tape. He used whatever was around him, didn't tape anyone up... didn't have to, they were dead long before they thought of themselves in trouble.

When his phone rang again, he pulled it out and answered without looking at the ID. It was Carson...he was the only one that would continue to call if you didn't answer the first time. No matter what you were doing, Carson was first on your list. But it wasn't him.

"Something else you should know. I'm so forgetful sometimes, I even amaze myself that I get around to finding my man. Don't you think that is a bad trait for a man in my business? Anyway, I forgot to tell you that you're not to leave town. Not until I say you can. If you try, even in that private jet you have sitting at the Columbus Airport, then you'll be arrested. And once I have you in custody, you're there for good."

Closing the phone when the man laughed again, Blaine couldn't think beyond the screaming ring in his head.

"Mother fuck." Yes, that about summed it up.

The next phone call was from Carson. And he decided right then and there he wasn't going to marry his bitch of a daughter and he was going to get the fuck out of town now, while he thought he could. So instead of telling him what he'd just done and said, he listened as Carson threatened him with every kind of death he could think of. Blaine was so fucked right now.

~~~

Gabe liked his home. He'd just purchased it about three months ago, and had only moved in last week. Renovations were still ongoing. He had enlarged the kitchen and updated

59

it. There was work being done on the fireplace as well. He didn't want to chop wood, so he'd had an insert put in. Just small things that were necessary and some that weren't.

"This is a nice room." He nodded at Rayne, knowing that she came from money and would see his novice attempts at making this house a home. "You've been doing it all yourself?"

"No, I'm not that stupid, nor that handy with a hammer. No, I have a friend that is coming in and doing the work after he gets off his regular job. He's a teacher by trade, but he loves to do this sort of work on the side." Rayne told him he should convince his friend to open his own business. "I've tired, trust me. He's set on retiring as a teacher. And he said that this pays the bills and gives him the chance to relax too."

Rayne looked around the dining room that they'd finished yesterday, and he did as well. "I love the built-ins you have in here. The way that they don't interfere with the flow of the room." Gabe nodded. "You did this with your large family in mind."

"To be honest with you, all we did in here was put in bigger windows after enlarging the room. All the cabinets were here when I bought the place. They were filled with all kinds of dishware and silver that I'm not sure what to do with." She asked if the boxes on the floor where it. "Yes, if you want them, we can use them. I didn't know if they were worth much or just every day."

"These are very old." He got down on the floor with her when she pulled out the top plate. "I love the pattern too. When I was hunting for things to put in my home after moving out, I saw a few pieces of this. They went for a great deal of money."

"There are twenty-four place settings of it." She looked

at him, wide-eyed. "I kid you not. There are even starter sets, as my mom called them, as well as glasses and other pieces. I think I counted over two hundred pieces to it."

"And they just left them here?" He told her how he'd gotten the house in a foreclosure. "And the furniture and things came with it, right?"

"It did. But for the most part, I tossed some of the soft goods out. The house had been sitting here for a while, and there were things that didn't do well with no one to tend to them. The table that was in here is being redone, as well as the chairs. It fit this room tight, but with the expansion of it, I think it'll work out well." He thought of the other things that were being repurposed, and wondered if she'd think he was cheap or something. "Whatever you don't like or don't want, you can just get rid of it. This is my first home. I've lived in an apartment since I moved out of my parents' house."

"Why would you think I'd want to do that?" He shrugged. "I love what you've done here. And I think that you've done a fantastic job. But as for me doing anything to this house, I think we need to talk about where you and I go from here. We're a couple, I understand that, but you have to know that I'm unsure about just as much as you seem to be."

"Your father?" Rayne nodded. "And...You talk to ghosts. That...I'm not freaked out about it, but it will take getting used to. I wonder if there are any in this house. They come to you, correct?"

"Yes, and you should learn what to do when they do. I don't know if you'll be able to see them all the time...I have no idea why, but they have rules, the dead. Just like we do. You can't help them out by telling them, you have to listen. You seemed to have understood that, but even if you know them, you must act as if you don't. Sometimes they have no idea that they're dead yet." He asked her why not. "I don't know. The tragic ones, like people who die in their sleep or a very quick bad accident, they might only think that they've been unconscious. Once they figure it out, without being told, things go better."

"I'm sorry you have to go through this." Rayne told him it wasn't anything to be sorry for, she actually enjoyed helping them, sometimes even finding them. "You do get to see your mom. I'm sorry, do you know how she died?"

"She won't tell me." Gabe wasn't sure how that worked, but didn't comment. "She said that it's not important, that we're together and that's all that matters. So, I think my dad killed her."

Gabe looked around the room, wondering if she was here with them. Was she telling her daughter that she was wrong? Did he really kill her and she was covering for him? Gabe had never met the woman, but he'd bet anything that she was protecting Rayne.

When she put the plate back in the box, they both stood up.

"Would you like to see the rest of the house with me?" He nodded. "I'm sorry. I didn't mean to bring my problems into this, whatever it is we have."

"Your problems are mine now, and vice versa." He pulled her into his arms and held her. It occurred to him that he'd not held her like this before, that she was his mate, and that he'd not kissed her either. Lifting her face up to look into her eyes, he smiled at her. "I'd very much like to kiss you right now. And hold you a little closer. Touch you in ways that my wolf would be happy about."

"I'd like that too. I have no idea why and this is going too fast for me, but I think I like it, and you." He kissed her gently on the mouth. "I think we can do better than that, don't you?"

"Oh yes. We can and will." Taking her mouth, he tasted what he hadn't in the first kiss. Her desire for him, her innocence as well. Cupping her ass, he lifted her higher to cradle his cock within her folds, her breasts to his chest. And when she wrapped her legs around his waist, he took her to the wall and then stopped. "Please tell me that we're alone."

She giggled and he felt his own mouth turn up at the corners. "Yes, my mom suddenly had a great many things to do, and there is no one else in here."

That was all he needed to hear before he moved them out of the dining room and up the stairs. He wanted her, and he wasn't going to take her on the floor or, even as much as it appealed to him, the wall their first time together.

He was glad as soon as he walked into their bedroom that he'd cleaned up after himself today. Usually he was called away in the middle of the night for things like deliveries and such, but since he'd gone out on his own, he'd not had any of those and found that he enjoyed making his own bed before starting his day, as well as his laundry picked up.

He didn't want to tear her clothing off, but he found himself doing just that. Her bra was shoved up over her beautiful breasts, and he suckled at one tip while he tore at his own pants and shirt. Gabe had lost his shoe somewhere between the dining room and the bedroom, but he didn't care. She was his. Rayne was going to be with him for the rest of his days.

"I love you." She kissed him before he could tell her that he loved her as well. "Hurry, Gabriel. Please, I need you."

63

"Yes, I need you as well, and I so love you."

Her body was hot, her skin so soft that he found himself running his finger up and down her arm just to feel it. Her breasts were full but not overly large, just enough for him to fill his hands and his mouth with them. As he looked down her body, touching and seeing as much as he could, she begged him again to hurry.

"You're hurting me." He grinned, knowing full well that he was not. "Don't give me that look. If you don't think I'm hurting here, let me show you."

Gabe found himself on his back, her body over his. And when she moved along his cock, her juices allowing her to slide up and down him, he lifted her up and held himself for her. He wanted her to ride him with him inside of her. As soon as she came down on him, Gabe felt his heart ache for her when she screamed.

"I'm so sorry, I'm so sorry." She nodded and he held her to him. "I should have thought. I wasn't thinking beyond having you enjoy yourself. I'm so, so—"

"Hush." He closed his mouth and looked up at her, and tried hard not to grin. "You are by far the most…Well, I don't know what you are, but you are the best at it. Now, let me adjust here. You feel good, but I didn't think about the pain either."

"I love being the best for you." She growled and his wolf did too. "He loves you as well. To think that you belong to both of us and…holy fucking Christ."

She took him. There was no other way to describe it but that she moved her body along his, her hips gyrating in a way that made his entire body sit up and take notice. And as she continued to "adjust," as she called it, his body ached to join her.

"Help me, Gabriel, I need to come." He rolled her to her back, and with her legs wrapped around him, he felt like he could easily die right now. "Please?"

"For you, anything." He took her gently, filling her over and over as he touched her skin, suckled at her breast, and nibbled on her throat. And when she cried out that she was coming, he was thrilled to know that he would be the first and the last to have brought her here.

Mark her, his wolf told him. And when he came, his balls achingly full, Gabe licked along her throat and bit down hard. Yes, his wolf told him, you've done well.

The taste of her blood filled his mouth. When she came again, joining him in their leap to the end, he moved her mouth to his throat and begged her to bite him. With the feeling of being torn open, her teeth marking him as her own, he came hard, darkness swallowing him up as he emptied himself deep within his mate.

Chapter 5

Anna sat in the corner of the big room and waited. She'd known that eventually the man she was looking for would show up. She'd been told that he was looking for her as well, but today, she was going to talk to him. Anna was sure that he could help her, but she didn't want to think about him being hurt again. And she knew that he would be. Just as she had been by her husband. When he appeared in front of her, his face ruined beyond what she had been told, she tried not to reach out to touch him.

"They say that Rayne is the one that can help us. That you and she can do more than any other has done for our kind." She nodded, then shook her head. "I see. Clear as ever, aren't you, my love?"

"I've missed you." He nodded and put out his hand. They couldn't touch, not ever again, but she laid her hand over where his was. "You know that I had nothing to do with what happened, don't you, Jim?"

"I do, and when I heard of your passing, I grieved for

weeks after. I've been looking for you since." She told him that she was trying to avoid people she knew, afraid that they'd think she was still with Carson. "Carson did this to you, didn't he? Just as he's done this to me."

"He shoved me down the stairs. I wasn't holding my daughter, thankfully, but he has been cruel to her since. He knows, you see." Jim nodded, and said he had figured as much. "I never told him. I never said a word to him about us, but he found out from that monster, Blaine Kline. As you know, he didn't take it all that well. I'm so sorry, Jim. I thought I was very careful with our meetings."

"I think we both knew that he'd find out sooner or later. And I have talked to some of his women here. They're a mess. To think that he's been allowed to do such a thing for so long and no one has tried to end his life." Jim laughed a little. "Once he is on this side, he'll not last long. They're planning a welcoming party for him. I'm thinking they have it in their head that he'll be here soon enough."

"I've been near him of late. Yes, I think you're right. He's been visited by a friend of the family that Rayne is with now. Such a lovely family. You'd like them very much." He nodded and said he knew the Winchester line. "Good. This man—his name isn't one I know, but I don't know the living well—he works for the Federal government. He paid Blaine Junior a visit and told him that they knew all his bad deeds. I think they also might have told his dad, as well as Carson. That won't go over well either. They'll either one kill him for that."

"I don't care so long as he can't hurt you or Rayne anymore. Did you help them find them?" Anna said that she had, but only a small push. "Good for you. You have always been the smart one. I love you dearly, Anna."

"And I you, Jim. You should see Rayne. She's so beautiful that it hurts my heart to think that Carson has been so terrible with her. And now he knows that she can help with the dead, he's going after her and sending Blaine. He wants her to marry him to keep her in line. I don't think that will be possible on his terms—Rayne is very willful—but he'll hurt her." Jim looked as shocked as she'd been feeling about it. "Carson is going to force them to marry, not that Blaine is objecting. Carson is going to pay him well. But he has also given Blaine permission, as well as payment, to keep her in line. And we both know what sort of means he will use to break her."

"You wish for my help. I have to tell you, I had thought you'd come to me before this." She said that she felt guilty about him being murdered. "It wasn't your fault, Anna. I was sloppy and got us both here. I will never forgive myself for that."

"There is nothing to forgive. To be honest with you, I think that he would have done so anyway, without finding out about you. The doctor told him that I couldn't have another child, and since I'd not given him a son, he felt my usefulness was gone. But I've been keeping other women from his bed as well. It's been a game for me, to scare them so badly by giving them little glimpses of his manners and ways."

They both laughed. It felt good, after all this time, to not just have a conversation with Jim, but to enjoy not having to sneak around. It had been too long, and she had missed him. She thought of him as a younger man.

"You have always been the best of brothers, Jim. I know that keeping you a secret allowed us both to be safe for a time. But, as you said, we should have known he'd find out sooner or later. Being forced to marry him...Father did all of us so

69

wrong in that." Jim nodded and told her again that he loved her. "I'm so sorry, sorrier every day."

"Don't be. Hiding the fact that we were related was Father's idea as well. He wanted the best of both worlds. A son that could tell him when he was about to be in trouble, and a daughter married to one of the richest, most powerful men in the world. He had his cake and ate it too." Anna said she'd never forgive Father for that. "No, and when I finally find him here, which I'm sure that I will soon enough, I'm going to make sure daily that he remembers what he made happen to us. I still don't know why he's not been killed for this."

"Me either. I'm assuming that he's had his hand in enough projects with Carson that he's not able to just have him come up dead. Father was very good at covering his own ass and letting others hang out in the wind." Jim laughed with her. "Carson is after Rayne. I need help watching her and the family that she's a part of."

"Her mate." Anna nodded. "They'll do everything they can and then some to keep her out of his reach. But, yes, I'm concerned about how much they'll lose too. I should like to meet the young man. I'm assuming that you speak to him through Rayne."

"Yes, she's very powerful at what she does for us. I don't know why she can do some of the things that she can do. I think it might have to do with the fact that she is willing to help them and they've made her stronger for it. Or it might be me. I've been giving her a little of myself when I can." He asked her about the mate and his feelings. "His name is Gabriel, and he seems to be all right with her abilities. Just today he helped her with a man he knew, and she was proud

70

of him for his input without breaking the rules."

"I'm glad to hear that. I truly am." She wanted to hug her brother. Tell him how much she loved and missed him, but he was a man of action, and bringing up how much she needed him would hurt them both more than they already were. "All right. What is your plan? I'm assuming that you have one?"

"Yes, I want to drive Carson to the brink of madness." Jim, so like the one she knew before he'd been tragically taken from her, cocked a brow at her. "You'll like this. It's one of those plans like I had as a child. You know how we used to drive Mr. Williams crazy by popping in and out of the strangest places in his house and yard? Well, this will be something like that. But with objects of his."

They talked over the ins and outs of the plan. But occasionally Anna would check in with her daughter. Not that she didn't trust that Gabriel would keep her safe, but it had been her sole purpose for not moving on, to keep her daughter out of her father's world. And it was hard not to keep an eye on her after all this time.

As soon as Jim left her, she continued to sit in the chair. Anna remembered the day like it was only a few hours ago, and not nearly twenty-six years. She'd been in the nursery with her Rayne...rocking her to sleep was her most precious memory. But Carson had come home in a mood, and she'd gone out in the hall to tell him to be quiet.

"I will not be quiet in my own home, you moron. Who pays the bills here? I do, in the event that you didn't know that." She said Rayne was sleeping. "Fuck that child. Do I look like a man who gives a crap about how much sleep that kid gets? I don't. And as soon as you're able, you're going to give me a son, no matter what those doctors tell me. And if you die in the process, well, lucky me."

Carson had started toward the nursery and she blocked him. It was a mistake, but she had to make sure that he didn't hurt her little girl. He asked her what she thought she was doing.

"You'll not hurt her, Carson. She's all I have. Stay away from her and I'll consider having a second child for you." She saw the way his face screwed up, his anger coming to full blown monster. "Don't."

It was all she said before he backhanded her. The blow to her face caused her to blink out, but only for a second. When she stood, he came at her, his shoulder down. When he hit her in the belly, it was all she could do not to scream. That would bring the servants, and she'd learned the hard way that he'd hurt her more if they were witness to their "spats," as he called them.

Her body was hurting, more than it ever had when they fought. Standing up, she made her way to the stairs, determined to find something to end her life with him. He had to die. She'd had enough of all this trauma in her life. And she knew, as surely as she loved Rayne, she'd be subjected to it as well.

But she never made it down the stairs. Never even took the first step down before she felt him hit her once more, his body shoving hers. The first time her head hit the stair, she knew she was going to die. The feeling of her body being broken—ribs coming from her chest, her leg mangling up and the pain of that—was intense. In her final moments of falling and life, she had not just landed on the floor, but her neck was broken, her body spent. As she lay there, bleeding to death, all she could think about was her daughter.

~~~

Kelley felt out of place. He wasn't sure he'd ever felt that way before. It wasn't a feeling that he wanted to experience again. But he looked at the kids, his grandchildren, and tried his best to figure out what they wanted. Every question had been answered with "I don't know."

"Are you hungry?" He knew his own sons would have been. Ten minutes after getting up from the table, they'd be asking for something more. But these boys, he was pretty sure that they were still under a lot of stress and trauma. "Come on then. We'll go into town and see what sort of trouble we can get into."

The eight-year-old, Will, the oldest of Caleb's new family, just eyed him. He was the planner, Kelley had already figured that one out. He was also the one that the other two looked up to. Not just because he was older, but he acted old too. He had to win him over before the other two would be all right.

"What sort of trouble were you going to get us into? Quinn said we were to behave ourselves." He said that was a good thing to do, but his idea was for them to have fun. "We don't like fun. We don't want to cause anyone any trouble."

"Yes, fun is trouble." Kelley nodded, his heart breaking every time one of them would spout off a rule they'd been taught. The middle boy, Alex, would be the one that would caution them about these rules every time. "Momma said that if we were having fun, we weren't learning anything."

"Are you hungry?" The youngest, Tommy, nodded, then looked at his brothers. "Well, if you're not, I am. I had my heart set on some pizza and a soda. I know you can't have that, but today, we're having a no rule day."

Shock was written on Will's face, and Alex wasn't sure.

73

But Tommy was nodding again, like this was the best rule ever. Kelley was going to do this even if it killed him. They were his grandbabies, and he wanted them to like him.

They got into his new car and he made sure they were all buckled in. Tommy was still in one of those seat contraptions that took four hands and a lot of swear words to make work. But the other two knew how to do it, and soon they were on their way.

"What is pizza?" He glanced in the mirror at Alex. The five-year-old would break free occasionally and go out on his own, but not often. "I don't think it's something that is good for us."

"Sure it is. It's got meat and cheese, which is part of the food groups. And wheat too. The bread is called crust. Then there are some peppers. That's your veggies. Of course, we'll have to have some of the tomato sauce, and that'll be our fruit." He'd never thought of pizza as hitting all the food groups before, and he was proud of himself. "We might hold off on the soda until the next time we have some fun. Today, we'll have milk."

They pulled up in front of the restaurant, and he was almost relieved to see his son coming toward him. Gabe would know how to handle kids...he did work with them. But when he invited him to have a seat with them, he told him that he had to hurry back to the office.

"But, I can tell you that my dad is the best person to have some lunch with. He'll even pick up the bill." Gabe winked at him. "Dad, you have to take them to the yogurt place after this. They have a new flavor, it's all jelly bean."

"I can do that." When Gabe left, he looked at the boys. "What do you say, guys? Two large with extra meat?"

By the time the pizzas came, he was feeling all his fifty some years. The boys weren't like others. And he knew why too. They all did. When their parents were killed some months back, no one had known the kind of abuse the boys had been put through.

They'd been fed and clean. All of them were smart beyond their years, but they were cold. As far as they could tell, none of them, including their parents, had been very social. Alex had freaked out when he'd hugged him the first time, fearful that Kelley was going to strangle him.

Their parents had taught them that everyone was out to murder them, and that they were the only ones that would keep them safe. Ever. And when they died, leaving them to the pack to care for, Kelley was sure that even a pack of regular wolves, not just shifters, would have given up on them because they were so very hard to reach, but not Caleb or Quinn.

The pizzas were a great hit. Once he showed them not only how to eat it, but to blow on it first to cool off the cheese, they dug in like starved kids. Alex seemed to enjoy it the most, eating nearly an entire extra-large all on his own. But Tommy finished his pieces and the crust from his. Will looked like he'd been trying to hold in his excitement until the waitress came back to tell them that they were having a special.

"You buy one and you get to take one half-baked home." Will asked what half-baked was. "Well, I give you pizzas just like you ordered, and they're only partly done. Once you get them home or whenever, you can pop them in the oven and have a nice piping hot one in the comfort of your own home. That's the best way to have one, if you ask me."

After loading up with their pizzas, Kelley headed to the

ice cream place. He loved ice cream, but he was going to stick to the yogurt, which he was to understand was better for a person. Not that he cared, but he was trying to set a good example.

"You know how to do this?" He shook his head at Will. "Yeah, me either. And the instructions aren't very clear."

"We can wing it." Will just looked at him. "You have to trust me, kid. When I set my mind to something, I can make it happen."

He didn't believe him. Kelley could see it all over his face. So, grabbing up the bowls, he handed each of them the middle-sized ones. He was determined more than ever to be a good grandparent. Going to the machines, he looked at the nozzle that was on the front with the flavor on a card above it. He was going for the cheesecake supreme.

It came out of the dispenser much faster than he'd thought it might. When it wouldn't shut off, he stood there in horror as his feet and hands were covered in ice cold cheesecake flavoring. When he heard little Tommy laughing, Kelley couldn't help it, he did too, and all the while he was trying his best to shove it all back up on the darned thing. The cashier came running to him when he nearly fell in the mush.

They all got into helping then. It was the biggest free for all in who could be the least helpful and not fall he'd ever seen. As soon as Will fell, Kelley put out his hand to help him up and fell right on top of the child. They were both laughing so hard, neither of them could stand. He lay there, watching that poor cashier trying to stop the runaway ice cream while telling him it had happened before.

When all was said and done, he'd enjoyed his day with the boys. They had gotten all the ice cream they wanted, because the manager was very sorry that they were so messy. Kelley thought the boys liked that best of all, and they even got some coupons that gave them five more ice creams each for when they came back.

"We can walk home from here." Kelley asked Will why he'd want to do that. "Because you have a new car and we're not clean. Our momma taught us that cars are too expensive to be mussing up all the time. We'll just walk from here, and you can keep your car nice for whatever resale value is."

"Let me tell you something. All three of you. I don't care if you have dog dung on your feet, spiders in your pockets, or even a sticky mess of ice cream on you. You can go anywhere you want with me, and I'll enjoy having you there. Why, I don't need this big old thing. I only bought it so that I could take my grandboys out to lunch sometimes. Or go on a little trip to the zoo. This car is for you guys. You wanna mess it up, then we'll still have fun with it." Will gave him that look again, like no one was as stupid as he was. Kelley got down on his knees, eye level with them. "You're my grandsons now. All I have in the world, and I'm excited to have you here."

"But we're not really your grandchildren, Mr. Kelley. We are only staying with Caleb and Quinn until someone else wants us." He asked him who told him that. "The lady at the courthouse. She said we were temporary."

"Well, she fibbed to you. You're my grandsons. Nobody is going to hurt you or take you away from me and my family. You're with us." He asked about other grandkids. "What about them? You thinking that I'd give you up over them? Just 'cause you're not blood?"

"Yes sir. It's what we were told." Kelley decided he was going to hunt that woman down and show her a thing or two

77

about lying to kids. "She told us we were to be on our best behavior or no one would ever want us."

Kelley pulled the three of them to him and held them tight. He loved these boys, with all his heart, and it hurt for them. When Will wrapped his arms around him too, the other two did as well. Kelley was sure that he could have taken on the world just then, just on the power of the returning love he'd gotten.

Standing up, he wiped at his tears, not the least bit ashamed of having shed them. He handed his hanky to Tommy when he cried, and told him, all manly like, that he had ice cream in his eyes too. Will laughed.

It was like having his heart stroked with love when he did that. And soon, all four of them were laughing and crying. Kelley hugged them again as he helped load them up in the car. Reaching for his son and Quinn, he told them how the kids were a wee bit messy.

But did you have fun? He loved Quinn more than he had even seconds ago for her asking him that. *Kelley, I don't think those kids know how to have fun. You're a good role model for that.*

I'm hoping you mean that in a good way. She said that she did. *Good. There is something else you should know. And it might well explain why they've been so cold around us.*

He told them what the boys had said about the lady at the courthouse. Said how they were only with them on a temporary basis. Quinn was outraged, and Caleb was silent. That scared him more than the temper of his daughter-in-law.

Caleb might be a great artist and have his own business making little things look great, but he had a slow to burn temper that would take the socks right off your feet. And not even remove your shoes beforehand. He didn't want to be anywhere near the courthouse when he went down there. And Kelley had no doubt that he'd be taking care of it today, too.

Did they tell you her name? He told Caleb that he'd not asked, he'd been in a state of shock since. *Yes, well I can tell you right now, she will be too when I'm finished. Dad, thank you for today with them. Without you, there is no telling how much longer it would have taken us to break the ice with them.*

Kelley got them home, and was happy to see that Quinn was true to her word on how much she loved that they had fun rather than the state of their appearance. Telling them to go up and take a shower and change, she took the pizzas from him. He also handed over the coupons for the ice cream place.

"You keep them for the next time you want to have some boy time." He thanked her, and as he was turning to leave, she called out to him. "Thank you, Kelley. Today was special for all of us."

As he was getting in his car to go home, Will and the other two boys came running out of the house. He thought they'd forgotten something and was ready to help them look for it, but instead, they hugged him. Just wrapped him up in their little arms and held him tight. Will looked up at him and smiled.

"Thanks, Grandda. I had the best time today." The others said the same thing, and he found himself standing there well after they'd gone back inside. Kelley was a grandda.

Chapter 6

Carson was pissed. More than that, he thought, he was murderous. And he was going to kill both his daughter and that fucking ass Blaine. Where the fuck was he, and why the hell wasn't he doing what he'd paid him for? He looked over at Blaine's father and thought about starting his killing spree with this man.

"I don't know where he is, Carson. I've tried all his haunts. I even had the plane grounded so he'd not be able to go away on that either." Carson didn't believe him and told him that. "I'm not lying to you. I want this to work as badly as you do."

"Do you? I don't think you're seeing the whole picture here. I want her brought to heel. If any one of the men who owe me find out about her and what she believes she can do, I'll be next on the murder-for-hire list. They're going to be pissed enough as it is with the money gone, but her being able to talk to their dead, it's not going to go over well at all." Andrew, as Blaine Senior preferred to use his middle name, nodded, but didn't try to tell him again that he didn't know where his son was. "He talked to the Feds, did you know that? They sent me a little snippet of it, just to rub it in my face that anyone can be turned. I'm going to fucking kill him if he talked, so help me God."

"He didn't. He knows better." Carson didn't think he knew shit and said as much. "He knows that any word out about anything he might have learned in his life with us, it's going to bring him all kinds of hell."

"It'll kill him, is what it will do." Andrew nodded, not looking all that upset about his only son being put to death. "Did you know that he was talking to them? The Feds?"

"Hell no. I didn't think he'd be that stupid. He is, by the way, and a sadist." Carson told him he knew that part, that's why he'd made sure that he hooked up with his girl. "I've been cleaning up his messes since he first learned how to walk, it seems. I mean, there are so many deaths equated with him, it's beyond scary."

"I don't care about that." He didn't. And Carson knew enough about the man to know that he'd eventually kill Rayne, and that didn't bother him either. So long as he was able to get what he needed, if she indeed talked to the dead. "When he turns up, I want to know. If you talk to him, tell him to call me or else. And if I find out that you had any idea where he was all this time, I'm going to make what your son does to women look like child's play. Do I make myself understood?"

"Yes."

Not long after that, Andrew Kline left. The man was going to have to come up with a better answer than "I don't know" or he'd join his son. There were things going on right now that he needed to concentrate on, and not one of them was his daughter and her fucking so called abilities.

Carson leaned back in his chair and thought of his daughter. He didn't know anything about her. Not what she did to make money, where she lived now, or how she got around. Nothing.

The apartment that she'd been in a few months ago was empty now...all her belongings that he'd seen when he'd broken in were all gone. It had taken him almost three weeks to find her. And when he had, she'd not been there. Off on some trip, the landlord had told him. Trip? What sort of trip did a woman alone think she needed to go on?

Now, here he was back at zero. Nothing about the girl was predictable. She didn't even eat at nice restaurants...he'd had them watched. Nor did she own a car, not one that he could find registered to her. And whatever job she had, they must be paying her under the table, because as far as he could see, she'd not applied for any with her Social Security number.

Carson had thought she might have his money, but then dismissed that idea. She was a lot of things he found to be a pain in his ass, but she'd not take something that belonged to him. He didn't know why he thought that, but since she lived like a fucking hobo, he knew she didn't spend it if she did have it. Women, he knew, liked to spend other people's money.

Her mother hadn't either, now that he looked back on it. He thought about Anna all the time lately. How Rayne was so much like her. How she defied him. Made him angry at every little thing she did. Anna wasn't the kind of woman that he thought he might have married when he'd first started his empire. But she'd been a beauty and had told him no.

"No? Like that was going to stop me from getting what I wanted." He looked over at the picture of the two of them on their wedding day. It was there because he didn't want people to think he was a coldhearted bastard in not having a picture of his long dead wife. But mostly, it was there to remind him that she was gone and he was still here. Despite her telling him she'd see him dead before she would allow him to hurt Rayne.

He would never forget the day that she'd taken her deadly tumble down the stairs. With his help, of course. Carson knew that had he been able to repeat the day, he'd have done the same thing, tossing her down the stairs like the trash that she was. Her broken body at the bottom of the stairs had given him pleasant dreams for months after the funeral. For some reason, he never was bothered by Rayne again. No matter what he did to her, like going into her room to pinch her in the middle of the night, she would just stare up at him, as if she knew something he didn't.

There was movement just at the corner of his vision. Turning, he looked there, thinking that something had gotten into his home…a rodent or some flying thing. But as he stared in complete horror, a vase that had sat on his shelf for decades moved.

It had been a wedding gift from one of his lovers. Inside of it had been a phone number, as well as an open invitation to her home. As it floated above the floor he reached into his desk drawer to pull out his gun, just as the vase and its contents came crashing against the wall not a foot from where he sat.

"Mother fuck." He leapt from his seat and stared at the mess. If it had hit him, it would have knocked him out. Standing there, he turned and fired when the door behind him opened. His secretary of twenty-five years clutched his bleeding chest and fell to the floor. "Mother fucking dick shit."

Carson sat down hard, but he didn't put his gun away just yet. What the hell was going on? What the fuck was he going to do about this new development? He looked around, wondering if his wife had done it. But then he laughed a little…there was no such thing as ghosts.

The mess that had been made was cleared away. He had no idea what would become of the body, nor did he care. So long as it didn't come back to bite him in the ass, he didn't give a shit. But something had moved in here. The vase didn't just get up on its own and smash against the wall behind him.

"Anna? Is that you?" Nothing. He watched the things on his shelf and his desk, aiming his gun in the general direction of anything that might move. When he was satisfied that nothing was going to happen, he put the gun down. Not in the drawer, but on his desk for easy access should he need it. "Stupid wind."

He didn't even look at the windows that were barred shut. Nor at the lazy fan that he'd had installed a few months ago that he'd yet to turn on. There wasn't a breeze in the room, yet he was fine with blaming one for the incident.

It took him several minutes to settle back down. Getting to work, making sure that things were going the way he wanted them to, he didn't think any more of the incident. When his phone rang a few minutes before two in the afternoon, he stretched as he reached for it. He decided, just as he put the receiver to his ear, that he was going to find him a prostitute and have a good night of it.

"Hello, Carson." He said hello before he thought about it. The person at the other end could have been male or female for all he knew, so he waited for them to speak. "You don't know me, do you? You have no idea who is calling you."

"No, I don't. What the hell do you want?" The tisking reminded him of his late wife. Even after all this time, he could still hear her doing that when he did something wrong. Which, by his standards, wasn't as often as she did it. "Who is this? I demand that you tell me who this is."

Nothing. No reply, nor was there any more tisking. Just as he was putting the phone back in the cradle, the picture on his desk began to shake, then it fell over. He reached for it to set it upright when the screaming on the line made him drop the phone.

Carson stepped back, but the screaming could still be heard, and he knew who it was. It was Anna. She'd screamed just like that when he'd pushed her down the staircase that night.

The picture started to shake again, and no matter how many times he told himself not to touch it, he saw his hands, as if not attached to his body, reaching out. As soon as they touched it the screaming stopped and he paused. There was something very wrong going on right now, and he didn't like it. Picking up the picture, he screamed. Long and loudly.

Dropping the picture, he ran from the room. He knew now that no matter what happened he was never setting foot in there again. Not until he had someone come in and get rid of the ghost. The picture was no longer of a seemingly loving couple on their wedding day, but was now of him and his deceased wife, her body that of a long dead woman.

~~~

Rayne watched her mom laugh. It had been so long since she'd done it that Rayne was sure she'd lost the ability. But there was something she needed to ask her, and knew it would take her good humor away. She waited until she had a better grip on herself before she said her name.

"He killed you, didn't he?" She hated seeing the look of hurt on her face, but she needed to know. The screaming had scared her father, and her mom knew why. "Anna...Mom... did he kill you that night? Throw you down the stairs?"

Her uncle was there as well. Rayne had never met Uncle Jim, not in life, but she knew him well now. He'd come around about two days ago and had been there since. And though he couldn't see or hear Jim, Gabe was enjoying having him around too.

"He was angry with me. Not that I'm saying that I deserved it, but he was mad. He wanted a son. I didn't and couldn't give him one, so he was angry at me. Pissed, I guess you would say." Uncle Jim laughed a little. "I was going to leave him. Run away and take you with me, but I think he might have figured that no wife was better than one out there that knew some of his secrets. And I did, even going so far as to giving some of them to Jim. But he found that out as well, I guess."

"Father didn't know about Jim when you married?" Mom told her that he had a different last name, and that Carson had never put them together. "He thought you were lovers. I remember him saying that. That had you not fallen down the stairs, he would have killed you with your lover. I never knew what he meant until just now."

"I'm sure that he did, but he had no reason to think that. However, in your father's sick mind, there is always something nefarious going on against him." Rayne knew that. "So, when I died, I thought of you and how you'd be unprotected. I stayed behind. It was all I could do."

87

"And today? The screaming that you had me practice over and over, that's what he would have heard when you were killed?" Her mom nodded and looked sheepish. "What else did you do? Besides making me scream in the phone?"

"Jim was at your father's home. Jim is a bit stronger than I am, and he moved a few things around. It takes a great deal of anger or love to make that happen, and Jim is extremely mad at your father. Not just for our deaths, but for what he's doing to you." Rayne asked them what else was going on. "He knows you have the money."

"He knows or he thinks he knows?" Mom told her that he thought he knew. "Not that I care, but Jamie Winchell came to me a few days after the accident. He was sure that Father didn't have anything to do with it, but since he wasn't positive, he came to me. Jamie had heard from Father that I could see ghosts and thought he'd hunt for me. When he told me what he'd done, that the money was buried on the property, I went and got it."

"How much was it?" She looked at Gabe, forgetting that he was in the room with them. "I'm sure it's a great deal; how much? And what is it you plan to do with it?"

"Just under sixty million. And I have no plans for it other than to keep it from Father." Gabe nodded. "Do you have an idea how he might have gotten it? I mean, its blood money, so whatever you plan, so long as it's not to give it back to him, I'm for it."

"No, he won't get it back, but I do have a plan. I don't know how it will work out, but it will most assuredly let him know you have the money and that you can actually talk to the dead." She asked him what it was. "Hear me out, okay? What if you used the money to put a shelter in place for abused spouses and their children? An apartment complex that they can live in for free, or something that can keep them safe. I know that there are a lot of shifters that would roam around the grounds to keep the bad guys out."

"I love that idea." Rayne told her mom that she did too. "Ask him how he thought of that. I'm sure as a doctor, he sees his share of abuse."

"I do. A great deal of it." Rayne looked at Gabe, then her mom. "There was a woman in my office just yesterday whose husband knocked her around so much that she's going to be several weeks healing. She knows she has to leave him, but she's worried for the kids. They have four, and while he doesn't beat them, he still abuses them. And the three little boys that Caleb is raising? We're just finding out that they were abused as well. But not physically. Mental abuse can be worse if you ask me."

"He heard me." Rayne nodded at her mom, and then looked at Gabe, who was still pacing the room. "Did you know?"

"Know what?" Gabe stopped pacing and waited for her answer. Rayne looked at her uncle and nodded. "Rayne, what is it? Did something happen? Or are you just thinking this is a bad idea? It's just an idea. Seriously, I don't—"

"I'd like to help you," Jim floated closer to Rayne and continued. "I know some people that are good lawyers that will make it work." Gabe nodded. He looked at Rayne then back at Jim. "Yes, you can hear me. And I'm assuming that from where you're currently staring, you can see me as well."

"Yes." Gabe sat down, and then got up to sit in a chair rather than the floor. "I didn't even know...I mean, I heard you both, but it never...I'm talking with the dead right now, and I'm starting to freak out a little."

"Good. You should." Anna's voice was a bit shaky. Gabe looked at her when she continued. "I'm freaking out a little myself. How the hell do you suppose that's happening? Rayne?"

"I don't know." It was good that he could, but the reasons behind it frightened her a little too. She wondered if he could see anyone else or had heard any of the other ghosts that had been around. "Gabe?"

"I've never…If they were here recently, no, I've not seen or heard anyone. But then I've been in and out a lot the last couple of days with work." She nodded, and wondered where a ghost was when you needed them. Suddenly one came in the room with them, and she stood up and backed from him. "Rayne, do you know him?"

"Yes." She backed up when he came closer, his face full of fury. Her heart was pounding as he made his way to her. As angry as he was, he'd be able to hurt her. Only once, but it would be devastating. But before he could touch her, Uncle Jim took him down.

"She had him come after me." The ghost pointed an accusing finger at Rayne. "He's not going to stop until…He fucking killed me!" Rayne asked him who had. "Your dad. He called in favors and had me killed."

"No, he didn't, I did." They all turned to Uncle Jim. "I knew where you were, and knew what you were about. It wasn't anything for me to make a few people listen to me. You were planning to take my niece out, and that is not right."

"Niece? You're related to Carson?" Uncle Jim told him he was only related to his wife and daughter, not Carson himself. "Well, if that don't…That doesn't make it right that you had me murdered, damn it. I wasn't going to kill her myself. There are rules among my kind of killer. We never get our hands dirty when someone else is around to do it for us."

"That doesn't make it right either, dickhead." She felt her face heat up when he looked at her, but dammit, she was angry. "I still would have been dead because of you. And I like my life just the way it is, living and breathing."

"But I thought you were to marry Blaine Kline. Wasn't that what your father had in mind for you?" Sprintz shook his head at Gabe. "Who then?"

"No one is going to tell me who I marry or not. And it's a moot point now, anyway, isn't it? I mean, that ship has sailed." Gabe grinned. "This is neither the time nor the place for you to be charming."

"I mean, yeah, you were supposed to marry Blaine. By the way, he's a lot worse than I am when it comes to murdering someone." Sprintz glared at her uncle before continuing. "Anyway, Blaine's daddy hired me to kill you before the wedding. He was thinking that in his grief he could take over your dad's empire. And guess who he was going to make in charge of the hit team? Me, before you shits stepped in."

"So, you were working for Carson and were supposed to find Rayne to bring her back to her father to marry Blaine. Then Blaine's father hired you, for what I'm supposing is more money and perks, to kill her. But her uncle, her dead uncle, gets wind of this, somehow makes someone else murder you before you can his niece, and you're pissed off. You have any idea how stupid that sounds?" Rayne laughed, and Gabe looked at her before continuing. "I don't know why you're laughing. This idiot was going to murder you."

"Yes, he was. And you can hear him." He nodded, then

sat down. "Are you all right, Gabriel? Want me to get you a drink?"

"Alcohol doesn't affect my kind, but if it did, I'd be drinking the entire bottle. Anyone have any clue why I can hear and see what Rayne does?" They all shook their head at him. "Great. Something else to add to the weird ass shit going on here."

He didn't look upset about any of this. Well, not the hearing and seeing what she did part. But the rest, he was. When she sat down next to her, taking his hand into hers, she leaned her head on his shoulder as the rest of them argued and placed blame.

"Do you really think we should open up a shelter for abusive spouses?" He said that he'd been thinking on it since his patient had come in. "There would be a lot of money for it. I mean, sixty million, it would go a long way to making them safe, right?"

"Yes, in most of the circumstances that I see, they leave with nothing more than the shirts on their backs. None have money either; they aren't trusted with it, or there just simply isn't any. And I'm glad you understand that not only women are abused in a relationship. There are a lot of men out there as well." She said she'd seen it firsthand. "I suppose you would have. But they'd need clothing, furniture, even some medical help. I can do the latter of that, and I have a couple of friends that could help. And the pack that Caleb is now in charge of, they'd help as well."

She liked the idea and asked questions about what needed to be done. Sprintz was ordered from the house and wouldn't be able to return, and her uncle and mom went off to see about their work with her father. It was late when they made their way to their room.

Tomorrow was going to be a big day for her. She was meeting Quinn and Sara in town for lunch, then she was going to go and get the money that she'd had stashed away for some time now. A bunch of the pack was going to go with her. Rayne was excited to get going on the new shelter.

Chapter 7

Gabe rolled over and wrapped his arms around Rayne. She was warm and naked, a great combination as far as he was concerned. When she rolled to her back and looked up at him, Gabe fell in love with her all over again. Kissing her, letting her know how much he loved her, made him wonder what the next fifty or so years would bring for them.

She shifted again, bringing her body flush against his. Cupping her breast in his hand, Gabe nibbled a little, then looked up at her. Her smile took his breath away.

"I love you." Rayne told him that she loved him as well. "My wolf, he'd very much like to taste you. Lick you until you come down his throat as you do mine."

"Really? That sounds…Well, that sounds very sexy." He laughed and sat up on the bed, his cock hard and stretching from his body. "How about I make you come down my throat first? That way, when he's had his fill of me, you can take me."

His wolf didn't care for that and took him. Her laughter made him smile as she scolded his wolf. Gabe was sure that he was very sorry for not giving her what she wanted when she smacked him on the end of his nose.

"I don't know why you think you should always get your way, big guy, but in this room, we're in charge." His wolf whimpered. "From now on, if I want to take my human husband into my mouth and suck him dry, you're to behave yourself or not get any pussy. Is that what you want? No licking of me?"

Wolf laid his head down and covered his face with his paws. He'd never felt him do that before, and thought it was funny. But before he could figure out what was going to happen next, Rayne lay down on the bed with her legs spread wide. His wolf didn't move, but that didn't keep him from smelling her. Every drop of her hot juices.

"I'm going to tease you a little." He and the wolf watched her fingers slide in and out of her heat. "Yes. Oh my, you have no idea how this feels. Or how much better it would have felt had you not pissed me off. Your tongue would have felt so good here."

He whimpered again while she moved her hands over her body. As she cupped her breasts, he was salivating, her movements had him wanting to leap at her. But the wolf never moved, didn't lunge forward like he thought he would when such a delight was spread out before him.

"Eat me, wolfman." He did then, moving so quickly to take her pussy into his mouth that she screamed with it. The flooding of her juices made them want more. Fucking her with his tongue brought her over the edge at least a dozen times, each one more vocal than the last.

When Rayne finally pulled his head up from her body, she was covered in a fine sheen of sweat, her nipples red from her hands. When she told him to take her, the wolf let him go, just as if she had commanded him to do so. As a man, Gabe made his way up her body, biting her here and there. Suckling at her flesh when something drew his attention. When he was at her breasts, he took the entire heavy mass into his mouth and bit down. Not hard enough to draw blood, but he knew she'd be marked.

Sliding into her heat was like slipping into a warm bath; it surrounded him nicely. He felt whole again. Alive. Taking her, moving in and out of her slowly, he marveled at each expression on her face. Every time her body bowed up, it was to meet his downward strokes. And when she cried out, telling him that she loved him as she came, he nudged at her throat and bit down hard.

Blood filled his mouth. He swallowed twice before he could take a breath. Love, it poured from every part of her. Her blood was spiked with it, her touch made him feel treasured.

His own release was epic. Gabe was sure that he'd been wrung out, his body turned and twisted several times as he emptied inside her. And when she cried out a second time, her mouth at his throat, he tilted his head after cutting himself with his claw and commanding her to drink.

She'd done this before, drank from him, but not like this. This was...this was too much and not enough at the same time. His balls filled again, his cock stretched painfully inside her again. And when she sucked hard on the wound he'd made, Gabe cried out with his own second release even as she came with him.

Dropping atop her, he pulled her over him when he rolled to his back. He was drained. Gabe wasn't sure that he'd be able to even cover himself if he had to. As she laid there, he could hear her breathing, harsh as his own, his heart pounding like they'd gone on a long race. When she lifted her head to look at him, he smiled. Christ, he loved this woman with everything he had.

"You've made me late." He just grinned at her. "I'm supposed to be at your mom's in twenty minutes. I still have to shower and brush my hair, and then get dressed. You, my dear sir, are going to take full blame for this, or I'll tell her why I'm late. I might anyway."

"She'll understand. And she will more than likely not ask because she'll know anyway." That earned him a smack to his chest as she stood up. Rolling to his side, he watched her gather her things up from their room and go into the bathroom. He followed her. "We still need to get a few things for the house. How about you make a list of what you think we need and I'll give you mine, and as soon as this thing with your dad is over, we'll go shopping."

"I have to get some clothing too. I mean, I could order it online, but I'm not any more an online shopper than I am a mall shopper." He told her he was the same way as he brushed his teeth while she washed her hair. "Also, I've been thinking about this shelter. I think it would bring home the fact that I found the money by calling it the Anna McFarland House. I mean, what better way to rub it in his face than that?"

"I love that idea. But you must promise me that you'll be careful. I mean, even though he has no idea that you have the money for sure, he's still out there and still pissed off." She said she would, and when she turned off the water, he handed her a towel. "I also want you to think about me changing you into a wolf. I don't know if it'll hurt your ability to help the dead, but since I'm able to see them now, I would think you'd be all right."

"I want that as well. Quinn said that it's not that bad, the change. Painful, but you wake up so refreshed." He told her that he needed to talk to Caleb first, as he had to approve it, but it would be fine. "I'm thinking sooner rather than later with this. I want to have the best advantage when it comes to my father. I need to be able to know that he won't be able to hurt me like he did before."

"You let me know when you're ready and we'll do it. You will be down for a few days. Your body has to adjust to the change and everything, but if you've talked to Quinn, you know that." She said that she did. "Before I forget to tell you, I have four new patients today. So, I might be a little late getting home. Mom said she'd make sure you were safe too, but I want you to be extra careful. All right?"

"Yes, I promise. To be honest with you, I'm sort of nervous about going out today. I've been running and hiding for so long now that I feel excited too." He asked her what the plan was. "First, we're going to go to the mall. Your mom said that they were having a huge sale in the department store at the end of the mall. Maybe I can pick up some towels. Having two is nice, but we need more."

He knew that. But he was used to making do with what he had, and having more than two towels had seemed silly. But he could see her point too. What if someone needed to shower twice? There were other things like that as well. Sheets for the bed. Plates. Cups. He only had one each of those that his mom had given him when he moved in. There were the pretty ones in the other room, but they were just too...he supposed they were too fancy for him to be using for every day.

"I have an idea. You get us whatever you think we're

99

going to need. I wish I could go with you, but I have a full load today." She said she understood. "I've put your name on the credit cards already. So take mine, and when you're done, we'll have fun going through all your purchases. Maybe break a few of them in."

"Sex is all you think about." He wiggled his brows at her. "Yeah, that isn't as sexy as you think it might be. But I'll only get what we really need. When we buy for the house, I want you to be there too. Oh, and the china that was left here? It's worth some big bucks, but I'd really like to use it for us. If you don't mind."

"No, that's fine. I like it too. And it sort of suits the house." She agreed. "If you can find something to match it, like place mats or a pretty tablecloth, maybe you should get that. Just to brighten up the room a little."

After she left, he made his way to the kitchen, thinking about all the things that they did need to get. They had a house, not a home yet, and he was looking forward to making this one for them.

The knock at the door made him cautious. He knew that should it have been one of his family members, they would have come in. Going to the door, he thought about Anna and she appeared.

"I wasn't sure you'd come." He whispered what he was worried about. "I don't know who this would be, and if it's all the same to you, I'd like to not be hurt right now."

"I don't know her, but she doesn't seem to hold any ill will toward you or my daughter. I think she…This is going to sound very silly, but she smells of baked goods. Like apple pie and fresh bread. Could be what she has in her bag too." He opened the door and smiled. She was right, the woman did smell delicious.

"You're Dr. Winchester?" He nodded. "I know you. You've changed a bit, but I don't know your first name. I've talked to Owen and one called Dominic. He's a bit stiff, isn't he? Anyway, I'm looking for you, if you're Gabe. Ms. Carmen sent me. She said you might have need of a cook. I'm Abby Snow."

"Why would she...? Never mind. Come in, why don't you?" She came in and handed him the large bag that she was carrying. "This smells very good."

"She said I was to bring you some samples. You have a lovely home." He thanked her and showed her to the kitchen. "Oh my, this is wonderful. I can make this place sing with smells and food."

"Why did Carmen have you come here? Sorry, but usually we talk before sending someone out to our houses." She took off her coat and started pulling things from the cabinet and refrigerator. "I was just going to have some cereal."

"Cereal is for children. I'll make you something that'll stick to your bones." She pulled a large cast iron skillet out of her bag and put it on the stove as she continued. "She sent me here because I'm indebted to her. She doesn't think so, but I am all the same. And since she has not much use for my skills, here I am. I'm to tell you that she'll talk to you about it tonight, when the sun goes down. Here, have a seat. Do you think I could call you in a grocery order? I don't have a lot to work with here in the way of staples."

He'd not hired her. He had no idea why that was important to himself, but since it seemed a moot point, he thought it funny that she was acting like he had. When she placed a large platter of food in front of him, Gabe thought it

101

might be all right having someone cooking for them.

"I didn't have time for biscuits, you being ready to head out and such. You and the missus, you have any special likes, other than you being a wolf and all?" He told her between bites that he didn't eat much in the way of sweets or lettuce. "Yes, I can see that. The missus might, I bet. For now, anyway."

"You seem to know a great deal about us. Did Carmen tell you?" She shook her head and started cleaning her pots and pans. "Do I want to know why you have a lot of information about us?"

"Ten years ago, I lost my son. Not lost, but he was into some pretty heavy drugs and he died. I think, now that I've dealt with the harsh realities of life, that I'd lost him long before he finally passed. And one day, he did too much. I tried everything in my power to save him, but I just didn't have it. Then this doctor came along when I was at my lowest point and had a talk with me." She turned to look at him. "You told me that my son was going to do what he did no matter how much I wanted him not to. There were some people, people that were loved and taken care of, that just needed something more, something that we couldn't give them. You made me see that it wasn't my fault, and that you knew a group that would help me. Carmen, she was going to kill me that night. I had invited her to do so. But you saved me."

"I wish I could say that I remember that, but I don't. I'm glad that I was able to help you. You'd not believe—or perhaps you would—how many parents we lose because of their child dying of this epidemic." She smiled at him. "Abby, you don't have to come here and work for me out of some sense of obligation."

"I do owe you, but that's not why. Carmen saved me

again. She…well, you know her, and she can be intense when she has a mind to." He didn't ask her what she'd done; she'd share or not, it was going to be up to her. "David's birthday was the other week, he would have been twenty-one, and it hit me hard. Too hard, I guess, and I was going to take my own life again. She found me, cleaned me up, and not in the nicest of ways set me on my feet again. She told me that I needed purpose, and a job. So, here I am."

Gabe left for work after talking to her a bit more. He told her to have the grocery store bring her whatever she needed, or there was a truck in the garage that she could use if she wanted to go herself. He set her up to be able to charge it to his card, and kissed her on the cheek before leaving. Yes, he thought, having a cook was going to be very nice.

~~~

Rayne looked at the massive number of things in her cart. She was sure that Sara and Quinn were adding to hers when they found something. She was going to need a hauling van before they were finished, and they'd only been at it for just over two hours. Sara asked her if she was hungry yet.

"Yes, I didn't get any breakfast." She handed her two candy bars. "I don't usually eat candy, but I'm starving. You have a drink in that bag of yours?"

When she was handed a bottle of water, Rayne laughed. She surely did like this woman, and Quinn. They were both smart and friendly, and not at all like the people that she knew when she had lived with her father. They were stiff, and would never dream of going shopping on a sale day. She looked at the tablecloths that were also on sale.

"Is this going to be in that dining room with the pretty plates?" She told Quinn that it was. "I'd go with plain. You don't want to distract from the pattern on the dishes. I love that it was a part of the house, don't you?"

"Yes." She turned to look at her and paused. "Hmm, Quinn, have you heard what I can do? I mean, who I can talk to?"

"Yes, do you see one of them here?" She nodded and turned away. "Is it someone that I've met? I don't know that many dead people, but you never know."

She was joking, Rayne knew. And she was nervous around her, or the ghost. She didn't know who the couple was, but they were angry, and pissed off ghosts tended to be a little stronger than happy ones. Anna appeared beside Quinn when she was ready to confront them.

"They're the children's parents. The little boys that Caleb and Quinn are raising." Rayne nodded and glanced at Quinn. "They mean her harm, Rayne. They think that she should give the boys to them so they can be a family again."

"You mean kill them?" Her mom nodded and Rayne looked at Quinn, who was looking scared now. "Quinn, I need for you to stand still, all right? Don't try and run, it'll piss them off more."

"Yes, all right. Can I ask who it is, and who do they want dead?" Her mom said to tell her, so she did. "They want me to kill my boys? Are they insane? Well, I guess that has been answered. Tell me what to do and I'll do it."

She would too, Rayne thought. No questions asked, she'd do it. Rayne looked at the couple and asked them what they wanted. They couldn't hear her mom, nor could they interact with her. Anna had never met or had any contact with them, so they couldn't see or talk to each other. The same with Quinn.

"We know who you are. You're that person that can talk to us. I want you to tell that woman there that we want our sons back. They need to be with their parents." Rayne asked them how that was supposed to work. "You know what I mean. We want them."

"It doesn't work that way. You tell me what you want or need. I answer questions you might have and help you." The woman, she thought her name was Rachel, said she wanted her boys with them. "Again, how will that work? You know what happened to you, don't you?"

"We're dead. It wasn't fair that we died without them. All you have to do is tell the boys what we want and we'll get them back." Again, she asked them how that was supposed to happen. "I want you to take them out and drown them. All three of them. They know — we've been talking with them and they know that's what we want, but the house is too secure for them to get out at night. Tell her to let them go."

She looked at Quinn. Rayne didn't want to tell her, but she knew that she had to. They were working against her and the boys, and it would cause them harm. Looking at her mom, she asked her to get the rules that she was given a long time ago. Then she spoke to Quinn and Sara, who had joined them.

"They've been talking with the boys in their sleep. That's the only time they can. Adults write it off as a bad dream, but children…." Sara cleared her throat. "Yes, all right. Anyway, she wants you to let them go out at night. That way she can guide them to the lake and let them drown."

"I'm sorry, what?" She told her what Rachel had said. "She's been trying to tell them to kill themselves so they can be a family again? Her own children? What sort of person does that? Who wants their children to drown themselves?

I'm not going to do it. You tell her that. In fact, point me to her and I'll fucking tell her to her dead sorry fucking face."

"I'm pretty sure that she heard you. She can't interact though. But as to why she might do this, well, sometimes they get messed up when they die. It's like they are usually rational people when they're alive, but their brains aren't the same after. It's as if they can't reason things out." She looked at her mom when she returned with the books. "I can banish them, both of them, and that is what I would do. But they'd never be able to return to speak with their children."

"What happens if you do that? I mean, other than not seeing the boys, what happens to them?" Rayne told her what she knew. "So, you banish them to the place of the unliving. What sort of place is that?"

"There is nothing there." Quinn looked confused, but she knew that Sara got it. "They'll have nothing, not even each other. The room is devoid of color and emotion. No one visits them, they have no interaction with people, dead or alive. They stay there forever."

"And you'd do this to them?" She said that she had before. "And you have no trouble doing it? What I mean is, this causes you no pain or heartache? I don't want you hurt either, Rayne. Not for this."

"If they stick around, they'll hurt the boys. Perhaps they'll never get them to go to the lake, but their lives will be hell." She wasn't explaining it well and tried again. "Imagine that you're a teenager, and you have this voice that is constantly telling you that you're not good enough. That you'd be happier dead. Okay, now try to make yourself ignore someone that you loved. Your mother forever telling you that you'd be better off with her. That death was the only way. You'd start looking for ways to end your life. Not to be with her, but to shut her up."

"Can you ask them once more if they'll leave my sons alone, that they're hurting them with this?" She turned to the couple who was now taunting a baby, making it cry. The frantic mother wasn't sure what was going on because she couldn't see what was making her little boy cry. When Rayne called them to her, they both came as if tied to a string that she'd yanked. "Tell them that I love them and don't want to see them harmed."

"You heard her. She wishes for you to go away and leave her boys alone." Her mom opened the book up and she read what was there to them. "You know these rules. You were told them when you crossed from living to dead, and understood that you were no longer alive."

"There is nothing in that book that says that we can't have our children with us." Rayne told her what the book said, how there was no harming the living that didn't cause their demise. No haunting someone simply because they thought that they could. "It doesn't apply to us. Those are our children, and we want them to die to live with us."

"You've left me no choice in this…you know that, don't you?" The husband looked at his wife, then at her, and nodded. "Do you too, know, what this means?"

"I want my children with me. No matter the cost to them. They're ours, and we want them safe." Rayne nodded and her mom stepped back. "What do you think you can do to us? We're already dead."

"You will leave this world and never return. You will abide by me because I am the death watcher. You have knowingly broken the laws of your kind. Not just caused harm to another, but to your own flesh. You are hereby banished to the place of the unliving."

The screams were the last she heard of them. Turning back to Sara and Quinn, she felt her belly roll and her head spin a little. Before she knew it, she was sitting on the floor with her head between her knees. She looked up once, only to have her head shoved back down.

"I'm all right." Quinn was cursing at her, telling her that she had lied about it not bothering her. "I'm not hurt, but it takes a bit out of me to do that."

"Death watcher? What the hell is that?" She looked up at Quinn. "Or is this something that I don't want to know about?"

"Probably not. If you freaked out with me being slightly lightheaded, I'd hate for you to know what my title means." Quinn nodded and helped her stand. "They won't bother your kids anymore."

Quinn stared at her for several seconds. Whatever was going through her head, Rayne thought that she didn't want to know that either. Once she seemed satisfied, Quinn thanked her and then changed the subject. Rayne needed a glass of juice, and wandered off to find some.

Chapter 8

Blaine wasn't having any luck getting out of town. Or the country, for that matter. He'd managed to make it to Zanesville, but no further than that. Christ, this was as downtrodden a place as he'd ever been in. That might be an exaggeration, but there certainly wasn't a nightlife for him to enjoy, and no one delivered anything but pizza and subs.

He had all the right paperwork, his passport, as well as cash. But it was as if they were looking for him at every turn just to fuck him up. Twice he'd been to the airport and that Fed had been there. As if he had a sixth sense as to when he was showing up or something.

Then there was the guy he'd chartered a plane from. He'd been on the thing, the doors closed, when the pilot came from the front and told him he couldn't go today, nor any other with him. And no matter how many times he asked, he never got a good reason as to why.

He knew that it had to be his dad. Or Carson. He'd run out on him, plain and simple. And now they were hunting him down like a dog and he was going to pay for it. The last time he'd spoken to his dad, he said that Carson knew he'd been talking to the Feds.

"But I didn't. I swear. This guy came to me and told me that he was going to tell Carson that I was working for him. I'm not." His own dad didn't believe him. "Dad, I've decided to leave the country. Things are just too hot for me here. I was wondering if you could help me out. Can you spot me some cash?"

"No." That was it, just no. To his only son. "You got yourself into this mess, and I'm going to wash my hands of you so I don't get myself pulled down with you. If you think you can run and hide from Carson, you go right ahead and give it your best shot. But as of the end of this call, I'm done." The line went dead and he was left to hear a tone that was a sight better than the one that he'd gotten from his own father. And after trying to call him for two days, he'd been told the phone number had been changed. Then a few days later, his phone stopped working too. Christ, it was one thing after another. And he was still stuck in this one-horse town without any support whatsoever.

Blaine looked up from the table he was sitting at and saw her, though he wasn't positive. Blaine had seen her, sure, but this woman looked different, like she had not a single care in the world and she was free. He didn't know where that thought had come from, but he found that it suited her. She was free of every little problem that might plague her. When he stood up, she looked in his direction.

Blaine wasn't sure who moved toward who first, but they were standing in the middle of the food court with people going by when he realized that she was beautiful. Simply gorgeous. When she smiled, he had no idea but he thought that she might have shined, or at the least glimmered a bit.

"What are you doing here, Blaine? I think you might be aware that there are people looking for you." He nodded and asked her if she'd sit with him. "No, I don't think so. I'm here with some friends and my future mother-in-law."

"You're getting married? Your dad sure worked fast. He said that he had it all set up that you and I were to wed. Which poor sucker did he get to take on your fucking odd assed shit?" Rayne told him that wasn't going to happen and that she was quite happy, more so, not to be marrying him. Drawing back his hand, he fell to the floor when he found his hand up behind his back. "What the fuck are you doing? I was told that I could teach you a few lessons."

"I don't think you'll be teaching me anything. But you ever try that again and I will rip your arm out of the socket, then beat you to death with it." He looked up at her and asked her if she'd be nicer to him if he was dead. "Doubtful. I'd just send you away and you'd not bother me anymore. I asked you, what are you doing here?"

He was let go and he nursed his arm while he made his way back to his drink and half eaten sandwich. When she sat across from him, he thought that from here he could hit her in the face, and she'd not be in any position to hurt him.

"You do and I'll kill you where you sit." The gun that was laid on the table surprised him, so he put both his hands there as well when she told him to. "Now, I want to know why you're not in hiding. I know for a fact that you have the Feds after you. As well as my father and yours. You looking to be put in a deep hole without a marker to show you've been here? If you'd like, I can help you with that arrangement.

Right now if you'd wait while I made some calls."

"You're awfully sassy. Your father told me you were a pain in the ass. Look, I've thought it over, and you need to marry me, Rayne. That way I can get your father off my back, mine too. What do you say?" She told him hell no. "You're not being fair. You aren't married, neither am I. We need to get married so we can live in relative peace. And so what if I have to knock you around a bit? You might even grow to like it as much as I do."

"No one enjoys you, Blaine. Only you, you sick fuck. As for marrying you? No thanks. Not in any way, shape, or form. I've seen your handiwork." He asked how she'd done that. "I talk to the dead, remember? I've seen a couple of the women you've beaten to death. And one you strangled. They are not happy with you, Blaine. What if I were to tell you that if I kill you, you could have all the fun you want with them again? I'm sure that they'd enjoy it more than they had before you killed them."

"I don't know what you're talking about." But he did, and was really surprised that she did too. "I suppose this thing about you talking to ghosts, it's supposed to make me afraid of you? It doesn't. I no more believe that you can do that than I do that I'm going to be killed by your father."

"Don't you? Well, Allison said that before you killed her, you tied her to the four-poster bed in her apartment. That you wore a cap over your head, and that you weren't all that large in the dick department. She didn't call it a dick, mind you…she said you had a tiny little twig and some shriveled up berries. Is that about right, Blaine?" He looked around, suddenly very nervous to be with her. "Becky, she says that same thing about your equipment. More like a toy set, but anyway, she told me that when you were fucking her with it, she wasn't sure you'd stuck it in her but for the condom rub. But other than the sorry size of your peter, they both said that you were a sadist as well as a murderer. Sad state of affairs, Blaine, when even the dead make fun of you."

He reached for her throat and felt the bite of the gun in the back of his head. He wasn't sure how she'd done that until someone spoke from behind him. Blaine felt his entire body seize up in terror.

"Let my wife go or I will blow a hole in your head that you can see through." He let her go, but he made sure that he cut her with his nails first. "You fucking bastard, what the hell are you thinking?"

"He only thinks with one thing, and that is currently too small for him to use it well." They both laughed at Rayne's attempt at a joke about him. "I thought you had to work today. Playing hooky?"

"I thought I'd come have some lunch with you, and Mom said you came here. I was thinking we could have some—"

"What the fuck are you going on about?" The gun dug deeper into his head. "You really going to shoot me? With a mall full of people?"

The problem was, there were only three others in the food court now. Even the staff behind the multitude of counters was busy elsewhere. And the three men? They were dressed in black suits, and the Fed that he'd been talking with was right in front of them.

"Hello, Blaine. I thought you and I would meet up again soon. Mrs. Winchester here was kind enough to let me know where you were so that I could call in the Feds." Blaine asked him what he meant, wasn't he a Fed? "Oh no. Whatever gave you that idea? I'm just a normal citizen making sure that this town is safe."

"You showed me your badge." The man said that no one was going to believe that. "But you did. You came to my room, flashed your badge at me, and said you were working for the federal government."

"Then tell me Blaine, what's my name? By law, we're supposed to give you that as well as showing you the badge to prove it. I'm sure that had a federal officer come to my room and showed me his badge, I'd certainly remember it." Blaine said that he'd shown him too fast. "Too fast, is it? Well, I'm not sure what to say about that. I would think that a man in your position would have demanded that I should slow down. These men are here to take you in."

Each of the men showed him their badge, timing it for a full minute and a half before they said their name and even spelled it for him. Like he could write it down with the strips on they'd used to put his hands behind his back. Blaine said he wanted a lawyer. Then he wanted to make a call. None of them moved to make that happen as one of them read his rights to him.

"What the hell are you arresting me for? I've done nothing wrong. I'm just sitting here, talking to my future wife and having some lunch." He turned to Rayne. "So help me, Rayne, if you don't fix this, I'm going to beat the living shit out of you."

"I'm not going to marry you. I don't care to save your ass, and so you know, your daddy has been notified, as well as my father, that you've been arrested. I'm sure that they'll have something really nice to say about that to you." He lunged at her and felt his arm snap when he was pulled back. "Poor

Blaine. However will you fight with anyone now? You have a small penis as well as a floppy arm. They'll more than likely call you floppy dick. I like that. Plain Blaine of the floppy body parts."

He could easily have killed her. Just snapped her neck and then pulled out his normal penis and pissed all over her head. His dick wasn't normal, it was huge. All the women thought so, he told himself. Then he realized what the fuck was going on. He was going to jail. And from the list that was being read to him, for a very long time too.

"I want to make a deal. I want to go on record as saying that I want to deal for my life behind bars on what I know about my father." No one moved. "I know a lot about her daddy too. Carson McFarland and Andrew Kline. Whatever you want to know, I'll tell you about it. I know a lot of shit about them both. A lot more than any of you fucks know about. Let me off and I'll tell you whatever you want to know."

He saw him then. The man that had waited on him at the sandwich shop. Blaine had thought he looked familiar but wasn't sure. But when he lifted a gun up, he remembered him. He worked for Carson McFarland as a hitman.

Before he could speak, to warn them about the man, he felt his head explode, his body fall back. Nothing registered in his body after that. Not even when he heard the second shot fired.

Blaine was dead before he hit the floor.

~~~

Carson sat at his desk, still holding his cell phone in his hand. It was done. Well, half of it was finished. The man had been killed before he could take out his daughter too. He wondered what was going to happen with Kline and their relationship now that he'd had his son killed.

"Mr. McFarland, you daughter is on the line." He asked his new secretary who it was again. "She said she was your daughter, Rayne McFarland Winchester."

"Winchester? I have no idea who that is." He picked up the phone, still barking at the man in the doorway. "What the hell do you think 'no calls' means? It doesn't mean for you to send in any fucking cunt that you deem worthy."

"So sad that you don't think your own child is worthy, don't you think, Daddy dearest?" Carson felt his balls tighten up. Her voice...it was like listening to her mother all over again. "Well, you failed again, but I'm sure that you're aware of that already. The man, William Poke, did kill off Blaine, but missed me by a mile. He was very accommodating in giving answers to my questions."

"William Poke? Never heard of him." She laughed and he looked around the room. Christ, she was sounding more like her mother every minute. "What do you want, Rayne? I assure you, there are a great many things I want from you."

"I have it, you know." He asked her what the hell she was talking about. "The money that Jamie Winchell took from you. All sixty million. Well, a little less than that. He did tell me that he had a few things that he'd wanted to do, such as buy himself a whole new identity. But I did want to tell you that the money is going for a very good cause. I'm going to open a shelter for abused adults and their children. It's going to be called the Anna McFarland House. What do you think?"

"I think you had better be kidding. Even with that, you know that I don't have a sense of humor where money is concerned. You return the money to me and I'll call off my dogs. You don't want to fuck with me on this, Rayne. I want my money." She laughed, and he wanted to go out, find her, and then murder her. "Where are you?"

"Like I'm going to share that with you. But I will give you a hint. I'm very close to you, Father. So are Mom and Uncle Jim." He looked around his office and decided that there was nothing there. That was until the drawer opened beside him and his gun flew across the room. "Did you plan on shooting up your office to find them? I think you should understand that you can't kill the dead since…well, you know…they're already dead. You've already done that to them, haven't you?"

"What the hell do you want? Money? I think you've taken quite enough of that, don't you? Did you want me to confess? I have nothing to confess to. Your mother fell down a flight of stairs one night when she got up and was disorientated. Your Uncle Jim? I have no idea what happened to him other than he was killed one night on his way to the store. Could have happened to anyone."

"Yes, it could have. But it didn't, did it? You shoved Mom down the stairs because she wanted you to be quiet while I slept. Not very fatherly of you, if you ask me. As for Uncle Jim, he worked for the Feds, and you didn't like that no one had told you before you married Mom. You should know that they have a lot more information on you than they did before you murdered them both. I've been helping the Feds where you're concerned. You and Mr. Kline." Stupidly, he asked her what she might have. "Well, I've been talking to some of your old business partners. They're not at all happy with the way things went down with you ending their business relationships. Also, and this is really funny, you have a couple of women here that swear that you shoved them down the stairs too. Is that how you end things? Just a nice tumble down the staircase?"

"I don't know what you're talking about." She laughed and he felt his temper shoot off. "Listen here, you're to shut up right this moment. I will not have you spreading lies about me. Where are you, Rayne? I want you to come to me this moment."

"Are there any stairs where you are, Daddy dearest?" He wished she was here with him right this moment. The little bitch was going to get hers. "Oh, Mom said to tell you that she'll see you soon."

The line went dead, and he sat there for several seconds just letting his temper cool. But every time he looked at the wall where the gun was sticking from the drywall, his temper would flare again.

Hanging up the phone as calmly as he could, Carson tried to think what he should do now. If even half of what she'd said she'd heard from his other business partners, or even his wife and her fucking brother, was true, he was in deep shit. He thought of all his options, and decided it was time for him to make a hasty exit. Standing up, he called for his car to be brought around.

"Mr. Kline is here to see you. If you don't mind me saying so, he looks as if he's been crying a great deal." Just what he needed, a grieving asshole at a time like this. "Also, sir, there is another call for you. He said that he is with the Federal Bureau of Investigations."

"Tell him I'm out." What to do with Kline? He didn't know, but told the secretary to tell him that he was going out as well. "And I'll call him when I return."

"You'll do no such thing. I'm here, and you're going to

answer a few questions right now. I know you well enough to understand what you'll do. Run. Well, not this time. My son has been killed." He told him he was sorry, but he really needed to leave. "I don't give a good rat's ass where you think you're going. They said that Poke told them that you were behind it. That you ordered the hit on my son."

"Think about it, Andrew…how was I to do that when I didn't have any idea where he was? If he was shot at the mall, then that's his own fault for pissing so many people off." Andrew looked at him hard. "There is nothing we can do about it now. You said yourself that he was a bad seed and that the world would be better off without him."

"I never said he was shot, Carson. Nor did I tell you that it was at the mall. I only told you that he was dead." Carson tried to think if Andrew had said anything about how he'd been killed. "You knew he was there, and you ordered Poke to kill him. Why would you do that? He was my son. Yes, I was angry with him, even wanted to see him get his comeuppance, but not dead. And certainly not by you."

"You don't know what you're talking about. You must have mentioned it, or how else would I have known?" Carson started to the wall where his gun was still hanging. "I'm on my way out, Andrew. As soon as I return, we'll have a nice long conversation about what we must do to strengthen our ties. Now that your son is gone, perhaps we can…What are you going to do with that?"

"I think I'd like to see you dead." The gun in his hand never wavered. "You had my son killed because he wouldn't heel to your demands. He rarely did mine either, but I would never had had him killed over it. Now you're going out of town. I'm assuming that you don't plan to return? Is that your plan?" He nodded before he thought that a lie would serve him better. The bullet to his shoulder took his breath away and he fell back. "That is for the pain and suffering that I've had to endure over the years because of you. Just to put up with you to make a little cash on the side."

"Andrew, let's talk about this. You know as well as I do that you can't trust anyone. I didn't have your son killed. It was just a lucky guess. That's it. A lucky guess." The second shot was in his leg; his knee was blown, and he knew as surely as he was sitting there he'd never be able to walk without a cane again. "Be reasonable. You can't kill me, Andrew. There are people here that will come in and see you, and you'll go to prison."

"No, I won't." The next bullet hit him in the gut. Carson looked down at his legs. The pain, all of it in his knee, was gone. He'd either hit him in the spine, or he was going into shock. "I don't care, you see. Whatever happens after you're dead will be a blessing to me."

"Don't kill me. Please, I beg of you. I've got so much to live for. So do you, Andrew. This isn't going to solve anything, you must know that. Please, just call an ambulance and I'll tell them an intruder came in and shot me all to hell." Andrew sat down in a chair and looked at him. "Look, killing me won't bring him back. Not that I had anything to do with his death, but I don't need to die over this."

"A few weeks ago I might have believed you. Even yesterday I might have, but there were too many details, too much information that Poke had about what he was to do. And you want to know what the really fucked up part is? Your daughter talked to him, spoke to Poke, and he told her everything that had happened and what had gotten him killed." He was going to kill his fucking daughter when he got out of this. "Carson, you're a horrible man. Just not worth having around. You killed your wife, tried to kill your own child, and now you did it to my son. Why? Because he didn't do what you told him to do."

"He was going to make a deal with the Feds. Tell them all about us. He told them that he had information on us that they would need." Andrew lifted the gun to his chin, and Carson thought for sure that he was going to kill himself rather than him. "Do it, Andrew. End your suffering before I do. Because as surely as I'm lying here in pain, you are going to regret — "

The next bullet ripped into his chest. He knew that if he hadn't hit his heart, it had come too close for anyone to save him. Lying back, Carson coughed twice, blood pouring from his lips as it bubbled up from his belly. Holding himself, trying to staunch the blood that was spilling out faster now, he looked at Andrew. The gun was at his own head now.

"I left a note at my home telling them that I was coming here to kill you. I also gave them my books. You might want to thank me for killing you, Carson. You would never have made it in prison." He smiled then. "See you in hell, Carson. I'll keep your seat warm."

The gun went off once more, blowing Andrew's brains out the back of his head and all up the wall behind him. Carson yelled for someone to come to him. Anyone. As he was fading out, he saw her. His wife.

"You've come to take me with you?" She shook her head and moved around the room. "Anna, you can't still be holding a grudge against me. You pissed me off. We're going to be spending a long time together now, the least we can do is be friends."

"No, we're not going to be together, Carson. As soon as you die, which will be very soon, you're going to pay for what you've done to a lot of people. They're waiting for you." He started screaming that she couldn't do this to him, that he was Carson McFarland. But her laughter was all he got, her laughter the last thing he heard.

Chapter 9

Gabe finished up with the autopsy and tossed his gloves in the biohazard can that was nearby. He had to count to ten, then another ten, before he could finish speaking to the two men that had come with him to monitor the procedure.

"Rose Delaney was sodomized and raped just prior to her death. There are indicators that make me believe this had been a long-term thing. Her cause of death is strangulation." Officer Charles asked about April. "April…April was eleven years old. And four weeks pregnant. She, too, had been raped just hours before her death, but she wasn't killed like her sister. She was alive when she was put into the bag, and she suffocated. Her body…Christ, her body was beaten badly, her arms and her left leg broken."

"Christ." Gabe nodded at Officer Charles and felt his belly roll. Just as he was ready to run, to be anywhere but here, April joined him in the room. "We have all we need to make the arrest, Dr. Winchester. Thank you for…well, thank you for helping us out. You can count on us to make sure that justice is served for these poor little lambs."

When they were gone, he covered both the bodies up and then went to the sink to wash up. He wasn't sure what to say to the little girl other than to tell her that he was very sorry. She smiled at him, and he sat on his desk to talk to her.

"I was with Rose when I knew you were here." He told her it was his job now to make sure she was taken care of. "Rose, she's so sad. But we found Momma. Rayne helped us with that. They can be together before they move on. I don't know what happens after that. Neither did Rayne."

"I don't know either, but I hope that it's a good thing. You and your family, you need it." She nodded and wandered over to the tables where her sister and she were laying. "You don't want to see that, honey. It's not good."

"I know." She didn't ask for him to pull the sheet back, and he stayed where he was. "I know of others that need help. I've been talking to them, just telling them what can be done for them. Rayne said not to force them to come to the two of you, but to let them think about it. She said I was pretty good at that part, not rushing people who need you and her."

"That's good. We'll do all we can." She nodded and moved around the room, sometimes through things, but mostly, she skirted the bigger pieces of equipment. "What are your plans now? I mean...well, I don't know what I mean, actually."

"I'm going to help. I won't be here for a long time, but I think I can help you." He asked her how. "Teach you the rules. Show you what you can do and not do for us. There are also a few that might wish to harm you. Those are the ones that have a hard time believing that they've died. I want to do the things like Anna did for Rayne. Did you know that Rayne is the death watcher?"

"I've heard that before, but I don't know what it means." She nodded as she moved back to him. "Are you allowed to tell me?"

"Oh yes, I can answer all your questions. You might not like the answers, but I can answer them. You have a lot, I think." He said that he did. "Death watchers, it's the only people on this earth that can hold the dead accountable. Like I was saying, there are rules that we must follow, just as you do as a doctor. And the watchers, what you and Rayne are, makes sure that those rules are enforced. There aren't as many breaking them now as there used to be, but sometimes you have to make an example."

"And how did she get this title? And why am I one as well?" She sat on the floor and he joined her, sitting across from her as she stared at him. "You don't want to tell me?"

"No, but I must. When she was but a child, not yet born, she was being strangled. Rayne knew she was dying and she called out for help. The watcher before her said that he'd help her live, but she must do his job. He had grown tired of it, and wished only to be a man again until his days were spent. So, he saved her, and when she was born, all knew that a new watcher had been born." Gabe thought of that. There were plot holes, as his brother said about movies sometimes, but he wasn't sure how to ask about them. "You're thinking that this cannot be right. That she was but a babe, correct?"

"Yes, how did she know to call out for a watcher? And how did she do that, without the ability to speak or to breathe?" She smiled again, and he could see that she was not only humoring him, but making fun too. "I'm a country doctor, and I know how babies work."

"Do you? I think you will learn a great deal now that you

125

can watch over the dead. But she could call out to him because he'd had his eye on her for some time. The cord wrapped around her neck was an accident, yes, but not solely. Her father was an evil man and he would do things to her host, her mother, that would cause them both pain. It took all the watcher's power to keep her safe so that she did not come too soon. You'll learn."

He thought he might. "So, other than enforcing the rules, what else will we do? I mean, with you, Rayne spoke to you, found you and Rose for the police." She nodded and told him there was so much more. "Like what?"

"Rayne, and you by extension, will banish the evil from our world. The world of death. The place of the unliving is... it is best described as a solitary place where the evil goes to be alone. They have no contact with their own kind. They cannot speak to anyone, nor can they do harm to the living." He asked her where she was if not the place of the unliving. "We stay with the living. Help them in daily things. Remind them to pick up milk, little details such as that. Sometimes we just sit with them, listen to them talk to their family and loved ones. Console them when they are depressed or saddened."

Something occurred to him. Standing up, he paced the large room. He wasn't sure how to ask this question, knowing that it was going to anger the little girl. But he couldn't get past the fact that she was just that, even though she had more knowledge than someone should that had been gone for such a short amount of time. Anna appeared in front of him, and he had to back up several steps before running through her. Her smile reminded him of his Rayne.

"You can ask her. She'll be able to answer you because of what she is." Gabe asked her what that was. "Someone that has knowledge to help you along your path. She has been given all that she needs to help you and Rayne. Just as I was for my own child." He looked at the little girl, then back at Anna. "We cannot speak to each other because we didn't know each other in our former life. She will speak to you, but only because of what you are to us all. Her sister and mother as well. But no one can speak to another ghost that they do not know."

"But I can talk to all of them? And with the help of April, I can understand the rules that they should know? This is all very strange to me. What if I see someone that died while in my care?" Anna told him that he'd know what to do when that time came. "You know, that's not very reassuring."

"You're going to do very well, Gabe. And I know this because you love my daughter so much. It was all I wanted for her." She appeared so sad for a moment, then looked at him again. "I wish to tell you something that you cannot share with Rayne just yet. Her father is dying. Right now he is bleeding to death on the floor of his home. I had hoped to make his life harder, scare him a bit more, but this, this is what he deserves. To die alone and slowly. I have a favor to ask of you. Would you take her out, give her some good times, so that this day is not marred by his death?"

"You think she'll be upset?" She said that it was her father, no matter what he'd done to her. "I can do that, but I don't think she'll care as much as you do. You loved him at one time, didn't you?"

"Oh yes. Very much so. Then after we got married he became what he is now, a monster with no remorse. He will pay for that as well." He asked her about changing Rayne into a wolf. "It has not mattered that you are one, has it?"

"Good point. All right. I'm about done here. I just have to fill out the last of the reports." He glanced over at April, who was looking at the medicine cabinet that he never understood why it was there. "She was brutalized. Worse than I think anyone knows. Even from what I've told them, I don't think they even know."

"She will eventually forget the pain of it, but not the trauma. It is what makes her what she has become." He nodded, thinking how some people should never have children. "Gabe, you will be very good at this. Just as you will be a great doctor now."

"How?" She just smiled at him. "What do you mean, I'll be a great doctor now? Does me being able to see and help ghosts affect what I can do now?"

"Yes." She moved to the wall where April was, but neither of them interacted with the other. "You will see soon enough. Go. Find your mate and have some fun with her."

He decided that he would find Anna later and demand that she tell him. Or maybe not. He had enough shit going on to last several lifetimes. Smiling, he finished up with the paperwork and made arrangements to have both of the little girls picked up by the funeral home. He told them to bill him for their service.

The second call he made was to have a marker made for the three of them. They hadn't found the mother yet, but he figured that they would soon enough. April told him that she'd been found, but he didn't know if that meant she'd been found by the police.

~~~

Owen sat still, watching over Rayne as she wandered around the wooded area behind Gabe's house. She'd been out there for over an hour when he'd come upon her. Now she seemed to be staring at nothing at all. He had no idea what was going on in her head, but he would bet that it had little to nothing to do with Gabe.

Have you seen Rayne? Owen smiled and told Gabe that he was keeping an eye on her. *She found out then?*

Found out what? He told him about her dad. *Oh, I don't know. She's been out here for a long time. I don't know if that's it or not, but she seems kind of down. I didn't bother her, but I think she could use you about now.*

I'm on my way home now. I was nearly finished up at the hospital, but got called in for an emergency with the little Ryan boy. He fell out of a tree again. Owen didn't say that was more than likely a load of crock, but Gabe seemed to know. *I've called Social Services. This is his fifth fall this month. I don't know which one of them is knocking the kid around, his dad or mom.*

I would say it's the mom. Dad is working a great deal, but that's only Ben's stepmother. I saw her with him at the grocery store the other week. She sure doesn't seem to like that kid all that much. Gabe thanked him. *No problem. While I'm talking to you, I have a favor to ask. Next month I'm going out of town. I was wondering if you could please pick up my mail and keep an eye on my place. I have to be at the auction house when the watches are sold off. Who knew there could be so much interest in some old timepieces?*

I would say that Mr. Cartwright did. Owen laughed. *I miss him. All the time. I think he would love seeing us with our mates coming to us.*

Yes, he would. But I can wait. I have too much going on. Gabe told him how he'd been thinking the same thing when Rayne came into his life. *I know you and Caleb are in love with your mates, but they're a lot of work. I mean, I'm barely making it right now with all the things I have going on. The house, then there's the money. Who knew that having so much of it was hard work?*

I know what you mean. But when you get back, I have a project that I want the rest of you to help out with. It's a shelter for abused adults and children. Rayne and I are starting it. He said he was in, no matter what he wanted him to do. *Thanks. Is she still out there? I just pulled in the driveway.*

Yes, but she looks sad, Gabe. Whatever is going on, it's got her really down. He said that he was going to play in the woods with her. *You should work on changing her. I believe it would go a long way to making her feel better about things. I think, when we go out running, she feels a little left out.*

I'm going to change her. I don't know if it'll be today or not. Owen said he should do it now, to give her something to look forward to. *You might be right. Anyway, we'll talk tomorrow night when we meet at Mom's for dinner. All right?*

Sure thing. Thanks.

Owen made his way back to his car where he'd left his clothes. He waved at Gabe when he went by him as his wolf on the other side of the garage. His brother and Rayne were happy, he knew that, and wished them all the luck in the world. But right now, he could barely wrap his mind around his life, much less someone else's.

Driving back to his place, he got out and stared at the size of his house. Whatever had he been thinking, buying one that was as big as a hotel? Well, he had it now, and thought that once the work was complete, he could settle down and get some of the little things he'd been putting off finished. Like maybe putting in a garden. Going fishing. Anything that would take his mind off life for a change. He missed Mr. Cartwright and the fishing trips they would take.

There was a lot going on at his house right now. Not just with the upgrades, but with things like the roof and grounds surrounding it. He'd been going through all the boxes that had been left behind too, and some of them had the strangest things in them.

One crate had several stacks of magazines in them, some of them from the early nineteen hundreds. He had been looking through a couple of the stories in one grouping that had prices of things from that year. In nineteen-hundred and one, they would sell an entire ladies' outfit for six dollars and ninety-five cents. Unbelievable.

There weren't any rat droppings or other rodents that he could see, so he was surprised to find everything packed away in excellent shape. Even the boxes of bed linens were in good shape. A little yellowed, but otherwise beautiful. Then there was the barn he'd discovered quite by chance in the wooded area behind his home.

Today he was going to go through the dozen or so trunks he'd found last night. They were in the loft of the barn, back behind the little bit of hay or straw that had been left behind. Owen was sure there wasn't much in them to keep, but he was going to enjoy looking through them as he had the many boxes that he was still unearthing. He was also planning to keep a few of them to put in the bedrooms for extra blankets and such after they were cleaned up.

He drove out to the barn after having a bit of dinner, ready to get started.

The first trunk he opened had him staring in awe. There were books. Not a few either. He'd bet that there were at least fifty in this one trunk. Pulling out a couple, he saw that they were first additions of some classics, some had even been signed. He couldn't wait to look up the authors when he got home.

The second contained kitchenware. He didn't know what all of it was used for, but he didn't care now. This was a step back in history for him, and he loved it. Setting the things back in the trunk, he reached for the third one. It was heavier, and he thought it was more books.

Upon opening the trunk, he sat back on his butt and wondered what the hell this was about. He picked up the first stack of money and thumbed through it. All one hundred dollar bills, bearing dates as far back as when paper money was introduced to the world. Eighteen sixty-two. There were four hundred stacks of hundreds, tens and twenties, and even some two dollar stacks too. If his math was right, he had just over eight million in the trunk. Closing it up, he pushed it to the back and sat there for a few moments just to breathe, almost afraid to open any more.

"This is insane." He didn't normally speak to himself, but he needed to calm down. Pulling the next trunk to him, he was relieved to find linens. Handstitched hand towels, small tea napkins like the ones his mom used at her afternoon women's club. Stacks upon stacks of them, some of them with fancy lettering, all stitched into them, not a single letter like he would have thought. Then he opened the next two trunks.

Tea cups that were so small that he couldn't put his finger through the handle, dozens of them, with little saucers. Some of them in small wooden boxes with beautiful paintings on the outside of them. Running his fingers over the top of a few, he was surprised to feel engraving as well. There were teapots to match most of them, along with dainty little plates for desserts or finger sandwiches. He found recipes for cucumber sandwiches in an old and faint handwriting that reminded him of his grandmother. There were others too, things that he was sure his mom would love to make. Setting them aside, he looked at the next trunk.

He was getting excited now, trying his best not to think of the money he'd found. He was sure, just by looking up some of the manufacturers of the cups and things, that he had a fortune in china alone. And it had been in this barn for who knew how long. He glanced at the money trunk before pulling the next one to him.

Pictures were inside, most in albums, others just laying loose inside. Very old pictures of the Eiffel Tower. Even some of the Statue of Liberty being built in the harbor. Owen pulled a few of them out, and saw that one of them had fallen down the side of the trunk. He ran his fingers along the seam, thinking it was a tear, and discovered a false bottom of sorts.

It took him twenty minutes to get all the pictures out. Stacking them up in a neat order had been hard, as they wanted to slip and slide over. There wasn't just old black and whites, but also tintypes and other older photograph paper as well. He let out a long breath when he thought what he might find under them.

"Holy fuck." He put the bottom to the side and stared at the contents. Owen didn't touch anything, but he was sure that he'd just hit the jackpot of all finds. If they were real. The necklace alone that he looked at first had to have been extremely expensive a long time ago. Today it would be priceless, he was sure.

The necklace had a large sapphire about the size of a small fist that was surrounded in what he thought were diamonds. Owen counted forty-four of them. The chain was a braided one of three different kinds of gems on each strand of white gold. He didn't know what all of them were, but recognized rubies and emeralds when he saw them. The clasp at the top was pearls, rough ones that looked to be polished to a very high sheen. Like whoever had made this had grown these for themselves.

There were other boxes of jewelry too, all of them velvet lined and beautifully displayed. Rings were in smaller boxes, all of them just as beautiful as the necklace. Bracelets and hair combs, two sets of pearl hairbrushes and mirrors. There were watches too, hung from long chains. The first one he picked up had a sentiment engraved on the back. It was a clue as to who might have left these things.

"'To my darling husband, Burton. Happy anniversary. Love, Birdie.'" Then the year of eighteen-eleven. He set it back in the box and looked at the others. There were six more of the same sized boxes in the bottom of the trunk.

After he had moved all the ones he'd opened to the side, making sure that he put the ones with the money, watches and jewelry somewhere in the middle, he started down the ladder to the lower level of the barn. Christ, what the hell was he supposed to do now? For sure he was going to ask his attorney about the contents of this building. Maybe, since he'd not remembered anyone mentioning it, it wasn't his.

As soon as he entered his home, he pulled out his cell phone with some of the pictures he'd taken while calling his attorney. The house phone, something he had to get used to, was ringing as he got his computer to come online.

He told Rogers that he'd discovered the barn and found some things in it. Owen didn't tell him what he'd found, but that he wanted to know about the contents or even if the barn was his.

"Yes, the barn is yours. I think I might have mentioned it…if not, I apologize. The contents weren't listed, but if you remember, you bought the property as is, so anything you might find is all yours. Including the well rights or anything else you might want to find there. I think at one time there were gas wells, but I don't know now. I can check on that for you, if you'd like." He told him that would be great. "While I have you on the phone, I wanted to ask you about the property next to yours. It's another forty acres, but it's occupied right now. An elderly man and his wife live there, but the land is up for sale. They would like to stay, just to live out their days, but that would be up to you. It's reasonable, if you want it. And we can buy it today if you wish."

"Yes, go ahead. And tell the couple that they can live there for as long as they want." Then Rogers asked about rent. "I know the couple…I see them in town all the time. They seem to be on a fixed budget."

"They are. I don't think the rent is much, but when you're retired as they both are, it's a lot to spend." Owen told Rogers to tell them no charge so long as they kept the house up. "That's very generous of you, Owen. I'm sure that they'll love that. I'll drive out there in the morning and let them know. As for the contents, it's yours. I just pulled up the seller's contract and it says that the barn is there but they have no wish for anything in it. So, happy hunting."

After hanging up, he looked up the names on the china. They were expensive and very rare, at least what he could find on them. The watches were another story, and he was too tired to look now. Making a note to do research later, he went upstairs. Owen had a lot do to over the next few days, and the

135

trunks would have to wait.

The trunks...he was going to move them to the house, but for now, they were fine where they were. They'd been there this long, he doubted that anyone would bother them now. Stripping down to his bare skin, he got into bed and closed his eyes. Not bad, he thought as he started falling asleep, for a little cleaning out of a big old barn.

Chapter 10

Gabe didn't want to disturb her, but he could tell that she was depressed. As he drew closer to her, he could hear her speaking. To whom, he had no idea, but when he saw the man, he paused in mid-step.

"My name is Rayne. My mother named me that because when I was born—"

The man was angry and he cut her off. "Why can't you just tell me where I am? I need answers." She asked him what questions he had. "I don't know. But I need you to answer them. Just tell me where I am."

"I can't do that. And you know that. What do you remember?" Gabe walked up behind her and put his arms around her waist. She continued to talk to the man in front of her, but she wrapped her hands into his and held him. "Do you know your name?"

"No, damn it. I told you that. You've hurt me somehow, and I want you to tell me what I need to know. There is something going on." Blaine looked around then back at

137

them. "How did I get here?"

Rayne repeated what she'd told him when he arrived. Her name, why she'd been called that, and her questions for him being here. Blaine was getting angrier by the minute. Then when it looked as if he was going to attack her, he stopped moving and started speaking.

"I was hurt. Someone shot me. I was talking to you and...I don't remember it all." He looked at him then...Gabe could see his mind working on something. "I don't know how I got here. Do I know you?"

"My name is Gabe Winchester. I'm a physician and coroner for the county. I've only been doing it for a few days, but they needed me and I—" Blaine asked him what his name was. "I can't tell you that. I think you know the rules."

"Rules? They don't really apply to me, do they?" He asked Blaine why not. "I don't know. Money? I have money, don't I?"

"What do you remember?" The growl that came from Blaine made him laugh. It was childish and sort of rumbly. Gabe asked him again what he remembered.

"I don't know shit, you mother fucker. Tell me." Gabe waited for him to understand they weren't going to give him answers. Taking Rayne's hand into his, he kissed the back of it and watched Blaine. "Don't do that. She doesn't belong to you. She's...I think she's mine."

"No, Rayne is my future wife. You remember that?" Blaine started pacing back and forth. Gabe spoke to Rayne through their link. *Are you all right? Have you been here with him for very long?*

No. Just a few minutes before you arrived. He's been trying to figure it out. I think he knows, he just doesn't want to admit it. To be killed like he was, it would be hard for him to grasp. He would bet so. Especially the way he'd been killed. *My father is dead too.*

I know. I wasn't going to say anything right now. I wanted to spend some time with you. I'm sorry, honey. Are you all right with that?

Before she could answer him, Blaine started talking again. "Someone hurt me while I was talking to you. The two of you." Neither of them said anything. "We were…there were Feds there. They were…I was shot and killed by your dad's hitman. I don't remember his name. I'm not sure I ever knew it. But he killed me when I was going to make a deal with the agents that were there. They were taking me away, arresting me for some stupid reason."

"I don't think it was stupid, but that's right. You were going to make a deal for your sentencing by telling what you know about your father and mine, and their businesses. Would you still like to do that?" Blaine just stared at her. "You could talk to us and we could relay information for you."

"I'm dead. I'm sure that going to prison isn't going to be an option for me, don't you think? Unless you know other ways for me to be imprisoned. You do, don't you?" Rayne nodded. "What? You sending me to hell? Perhaps to some place even worse than that?"

"Your father might want to see you." He frowned. "He's still wandering around trying to figure things out."

"You had my dad killed?" Gabe told him that he hadn't done a thing to him. Nor had Rayne. "But he's dead, while your father just walks around like nothing happened to us. You do know that he had me killed, don't you? Your father is a piece of shit, if you ask me."

"No one did, but you're right." Blaine started walking the

grounds again. "Do you know your name? Where you are?"

"I'm getting there, damn it." He paced more, his feet hitting the ground but nothing moving...not a twig broke nor a flower smashed under his footsteps. "I'm dead. I was killed by a hitman and my name is.... My father is Blaine Andrew Kline. I'm Blaine Junior. And I'm dead. I'm dead because your father hired some jackass to kill me. Why didn't he kill you?"

"I don't have any idea, but the rest of it, that's right." Rayne moved toward Blaine, but not close enough for him to touch her. Gabe waited, not sure what she had in mind. "You've been dead for three days now. In that time, you have been working to figure out where you were or what you needed. I can answer any questions you might have, but you must follow the rules of your kind."

"I told you, I'm not cut out for rules. And I don't want to be dead. Can you fix that? I mean, I've been an all right guy. Except for a few murders. A couple of rapes and some petty things that might be frowned upon. But I'm not sure that's enough to have me punished, do you?" Gabe wanted to laugh but held his tongue. "You can fix that for me, can't you, Rayne? I don't want to be dead. I'm much too handsome and young for that to be going on. Just change me back to one of the living and I'll be a better guy. I'll try, anyway. Fix this for me and I will give you everything I have. You must have some kind of power to make me alive again. I want you to do it. And if my dad is dead, I'm very wealthy. I can pay you whatever you want. Just do it now."

"You don't have anything, Blaine, and there is no fixing this for you. Dead, I'm afraid, is just that, dead. There will be no one to bring you back. And even if there was, which there isn't, you're not anything near being an all right guy. You're a murderer, a prick, and an asshole. But you have several choices that you can make, now that you understand, that — "

"The only choice that I want you to give me is the one where I'm alive and live out the rest of my days. This is bullshit. I didn't die at the right time in my life. I should have years and years to go yet. I won't take no for an answer. You fix this. I know you can." Gabe wanted to laugh. Blaine was acting like a small boy who hadn't had a nap yet. "You just do whatever it is that you need to and I'll wait right here. There isn't any reason that I have to be dead other than you don't like me."

"No, I don't like you. Not at all. But as I have said, I can't change the way things have ended up for you." Blaine started cursing, loud and long. "Yes, that's showing that you are going to try and change your ways. You have things you can do. You can either roam around here — "

"I'm not kidding you, Rayne. I am not going to be dead. You can't do this to me. This is all your fault...you have to fix this to make up for the fact that you had me killed, or your father did. So, fix me." Gabe asked what it was he thought that she'd done to him. "Everything. Christ, all she had to do was just be my wife. I would have gotten so much cash, and your dad wouldn't have had me killed. This is all your fault. I'm not going to take this shit from you. You will fix this for me."

"There is no fixing it. You're dead and that's the end of it. You either play by the rules that you were made aware of the moment you remembered who you were, or you don't. Either way, you will be held accountable for your actions. Much more so than you were when you were living." He snorted at her and Rayne looked at Gabe. "He's being stupid."

"I would say that is natural for him, wouldn't you? Being stupid, pigheaded, as well as thinking he's above such things as rules." Rayne smiled up at him. "There's my girl. What else can you do to make him aware of what is going to happen? I mean, does he have to sign anything?"

"No. Once someone that has died remembers their name, it's like this thing plugs into their head and they know the rules they must follow, as well as boundaries." He asked her what that meant. "Mom told me that it told them where they could go and where it was off limits to them. Some never understand that, while others simply don't care. I think that he's going to not care about any of this."

"He didn't in life, it's doubtful that—" Blaine let out a primal scream. It was very girly like, as if he was going to stomp his foot next. "Is there something wrong, Blaine? We were sure that we'd cleared everything up for you. Whatever could be making you pissed now? You are, aren't you?"

"Yes, I'm still dead, you mother fuckers. Fix this." Gabe told him that was what happened when you were shot in the head. "I'm not staying this way. You will make me alive again."

"Will we? Okay, you tell me how that is supposed to work and I'll think about it. Because from where I'm standing, you got just what you deserved. But if you have a plan that will erase the big fucking hole in your head, then you let me know how to fix it." He asked about the hole in his head. "You were shot there. Did you expect it to just not show up when you were dead? Get real. Most of your face is gone."

"No, I need that. When you bring me back from the dead, I'm going to need my looks too. Put that on the list of things you have to take care of." Gabe looked at Rayne as he continued to demand that they bring him back to life. "I'm also going to need something to wear that isn't stained like this one is. What is this anyway? It's all brownish and is dried hard. What the fuck is this on my three-thousand-dollar suit?"

"Blood." Leading Rayne away from the idiot was easy; getting him to shut up was harder. He kept telling them things he wanted, or better yet, what he demanded of them. By the time they were at the house again, Rayne was laughing as hard as he was. The man had a set of balls as small as his brain, it seemed.

"That's a first for me, and I've been doing this for a long time." She giggled again. "He is going to be trouble, I know it. I wonder why he thinks we'd even want to bring him back if we could. The man is a fool."

"He is a strange man, and I would think that he really does believe that rules shouldn't have to apply to him, simply because he has money. I don't ever want to feel that way." She moved to the couch and he stayed where he was. "I was planning on taking you out there in the woods, then perhaps changing you."

"You still can. I mean, not out there. He'll be hanging around for a little while, and asking him to leave would be the same as telling him to hang around." Gabe smiled at her. "My father is dead. I'm not sure how I feel about that."

"You should feel how you want to about it." She nodded, but didn't seem like she knew yet. "You loved him, I'm sure. And you were also pissed at him a great deal. Either of those are acceptable ways to feel about the man."

"He killed my mother. He might have me as well, if I hadn't had her there to keep me safe. Not really safe I guess, but quiet when he was in the house." Gabe started for her,

143

just to hold her when she stood up. "How does this work? The changing thing? I know that you have to bite me, but after that, what goes on?"

"Are you sure about this?" She nodded at him. "Well, before we do that, I'd very much like to make love to you. Take you upstairs and strip you — "

"Hard and dirty." He asked her what she meant. "You know, bend me over the back of this couch, take me hard, and then bite me. I want to feel you fucking me like you mean it."

His cock stretched in his pants, his heartrate doubled. Even his wolf, who was normally as calm as he was, perked up. It felt like he was telling him to get with the program and give their mate what she wanted. While he stood there with his tongue hanging out, she started to strip out of her clothing. Not using the buttons or the zipper, but ripping it off her in shreds.

"You're making me insane." She said that was the point. "I think I love this side of you. My wolf certainly does."

"Well, tell him to get over here and eat me." His wolf didn't need any other encouragement, but took him quickly. "That's it, big boy, bring me to peak and I'll make it worth your while."

~~~

Rayne wasn't sure what had gotten into her, but she was glad Gabe didn't make fun of her. As his wolf came toward her, moving like he was going to leap at his prey, she talked to him, told him all the things she wanted him to do to her. Both him and Gabe. Spreading her legs wide when he nudged her knees apart, Rayne cried out when his tongue touched her clit. Then she was shoved back on the couch behind her.

He ate her hard, nipping at her tender flesh several times

144

until she cried out with a release. Six times, six wonderfully erotic times he brought her, each time growling low in his throat when she begged him to stop.

"I can't take it anymore." Gabe told her that she could and she would. She'd awakened his beast and she was going to deal with him. "Please. I need you. Come inside of me, Gabriel."

Come for him. Satisfy him so that I can. Rayne came three more times, her body bowing up off the couch with each release while getting weaker each time. *You taste so good to him. He loves the way your cream slides down the back of his throat. The way you give him more with each time you come. Come for us, baby, give us what we want.*

She did, twice more, both powerful punches to her system that made her feel as if she'd been wrung out then run over. As she screamed out her next release, her body bathed in her own sweat, she begged once again for Gabriel to let her go.

The air around her tightened, making her realize that Gabriel was with her. If that wasn't enough, the feeling of the tongue deep inside of her changed. Just when she was thinking that she was finished, that she was going to faint from it all, Gabriel was between her legs, eating her like she was going to be his last meal. And he wasn't any easier to convince that she was worn out than his wolf had been.

"Gabriel, please. Fuck me." He told her no, he wasn't done yet. "But I am. It's too much. I can't—"

His finger sliding into her took her over the edge like she'd ever been before. Her thoughts were gone, her breath too. And when she let go of the climax, the scream that tore from her throat was painful. Her entire body felt like it had not just been stuck in an electrical socket, but that it had been

145

the highest wattage of voltage that she'd ever known.

There were shooting stars, butterflies, and rockets. And when she came back to herself, almost floating to the couch again, she knew she'd never be the same again. Then Gabriel filled her. His cock became a part of her. She held onto him while he took her to even greater heights than before.

"Come for us." She shook her head no. There wasn't anything left of her to give. "Come, Rayne, and I'll bite you."

She blacked out. Her body just simply closed down when the climax became too much. Dropping her arms to the side, she felt the moment that Gabriel came inside of her. And when he threw back his head and howled, the hairs on her arms and neck danced for the pure pleasure it gave her to know that he'd come with her.

The wolf was standing over her when she opened her eyes. Rayne had no idea how long she'd been out or when it had happened, but she reached for his neck to hold him to her when he lunged at her, tearing into her belly hard enough to bring tears and a small scream from her.

The big wolf tore at her belly. She knew that he'd broken several bones while he was doing the job of changing her. Rayne didn't care. It was happening. She would be a wolf just like Gabriel when this was finished.

The pain blurred in and out of her mind. She knew that Gabriel was talking to her. What he was saying, she didn't have any idea. Her entire being was focused on one thing...to get through this. To not die. When he bit into her leg, tearing into it as he had her belly, she didn't even have the strength to scream any more. The wolf whimpered when she put her hand on his back, but she was only offering comfort to him, not asking him to stop. The final time that he bit her, tearing into her arm where her upper arm met her shoulder, she fainted. It was too much for her to try and hang on any longer.

Rayne thought she was dead, waking in a room devoid of color. But when she sat up, not only did color fill the room, but flowers and birds were there as well. On some level, she knew that she wasn't dead, but she didn't know where she was. Unconscious, she finally figured out, and closed her eyes again.

"Rayne? Honey, can you hear me?" Opening her eyes, she looked at her mom and smiled. "There you go. I knew you'd be all right now. You're with me, just on the other side of life. You're going to be just fine."

"I'm going to be a wolf. Gabriel and I will be able to run and have so much fun now." Mom nodded and told her that they would. Forever. "How did I get here? Am I dead?"

"You were, but for only a moment. I've brought you here so that I could have you all to myself for a bit. I must talk to you. I know that you are going to be safe now." Rayne told her that they all would. "Yes, now that you have Gabe in your life and your father is dead, you'll be happy too. That's all I ever wanted for you. Safety and happiness."

"Mom? What's going on?" Rayne felt herself being moved. There wasn't enough energy for her to open her eyes yet in the real world, so she only looked at her mom. She was fading. Not just from color, but her body was translucent as well. "Mom?"

"It's time I moved on. I can't stay here any longer. I don't think I want to, now that you're safe." Rayne told her no, that she needed her. "No darling, you don't need me anymore. You have a love that will keep you happy. This was only temporary, you always knew that. You have Gabe now, and

147

I'm tired. So very tired, love."

"You have to stay with me, Mom. Don't you see? I can't do this job without you here." Her mom touched her fingers to her face and Rayne felt it. "Mom. You can't leave me. I need you in my life."

"No, Rayne. You did need me, but no longer. I'm going to move on. It's my time. I'm here telling you this now because I wanted to be able to touch you again, once more." Rayne buried her face into her mother's touch. "You were always the best child. No one could have ever asked for a better one. I will love you forever and more, Rayne. And you'll do right by all the ones that come after me. Gabe is a wonderful man, strong, and he loves you more than I ever could have hoped for. I love you, Rayne. With every bit of my heart."

"I love you too, Mom. Please don't leave me. What will I do without you here to guide me along? Who will help me when the others need me?" Mom told her that Gabriel would be there for her. "But I want you here…I need you here, Mom. You've always been here for me."

"I know, and in some ways, I think I was selfish for being here for you. I didn't want to move on and leave you alone. I needed you as much as, if not more than, you needed me. But it's not like that anymore. You're so happy that I feel like it's just what I was waiting for. You to have a love of your life that you deserve." Rayne wanted to beg her mom to stay with her, but she could see that she was indeed ready. "One day you'll have yourself a child, or several, and when you do, I want you to remember that you must let go sometimes to let them make their own way in the world. Like I am for you right now."

She slipped away from her. Just let go of her and faded

away. Rayne felt her body being warmed, her heart breaking yet feeling renewed. For some reason, she knew that Gabriel was close to her and that he was holding her tight. Calling for her mom to come back to her would be cruel, she knew, so Rayne let her body rest so that she could be the best wolf she could ever hope to be. Gabe spoke to her...she heard it as well as she had her mom calling to her.

"I love you, Rayne." She knew he did. Gabriel would love her forever too. "You are my heart, and when you wake, I'm going to marry you."

Yes, she thought, to be married to her best friend and her lover would be the greatest gift of all. Letting her body fall into the deep sleep that she knew that she needed, Rayne smiled. Yes, she would miss her mom, never go a day without thinking of her, but she was getting so much more.

Chapter 11

Caleb was just finishing up reading the contract for a new business when he glanced over at the bed. Rayne was sitting up, staring at him like she'd been there for a while. He slowly put the paperwork down and asked her if she was all right.

"Yes. Perfectly fine. How are you?" Caleb said he was good. "Did you know that you frown when you read? It's like you're pissed off at the words and don't want to insult it by saying anything."

"I don't care for the wording of some of the things in this, but I don't think I'm pissed at it." She nodded, and he thought she was humoring him. "You've been out for a few days; did you know that?"

"You are angry with it." Caleb leaned back in the seat and asked her why she still thought that. "Well, for one thing, you were cursing under your breath. I'm sure that I've heard those words before. By the way, is it normal to hear the bees in the yard making out?"

"Yes, you'll hear them farting too when they're done."

151

She smiled at him. "You can turn it down. It was something that Quinn had to get used to as well."

"She's nice. Too nice for the likes of you." He frowned at her. "I was kidding, Caleb. You and she are perfectly matched. Like bookends, or radial tires."

"Radial tires? Why...? You know what, I don't care. I'm only sitting here because it's my turn. You're supposed to be asleep for a couple more days." She asked him why. "I'm not sure there is a time limit on how long you rest, but you scared us a couple of times. Much like Quinn did when she was turned. So, how are you feeling?"

"Gabe said to tell you that you can go away now. He has to clean up and then he'll be home." Caleb said he'd wait until he was home. "All right. But I'm getting up. And I know for a fact that I'm naked. If you can handle that, so can I."

She threw back the covers and he leapt to his feet. As he closed the door behind him, he could hear her laughing. Caleb knew she was going to be just fine, but he wasn't leaving until Gabe got home from the hospital. He settled down in the kitchen with Abby, a plate of cookies, and a glass of milk.

"She's a nice young woman. I can see why the mister likes having her around." Caleb was shoving two more cookies in his mouth when Abby sat across from him. "I need to ask something of you. You being the alpha and all."

"Of course." He pushed the nearly empty plate across the table, and was both happy and sad that she refilled it for him. "Abby, what is it? When Howard has something to tell me, he tries to sweeten it with scones. While you might not be plying me with cookies for that reason, I can't help but feel your nervousness. Tell me and I can enjoy your cooking more."

"There is a rumor around that she can talk to the dead. Is

it true?" Assuming that she was talking about Rayne, he told her that it was, that both she and Gabe could. "I thought so. I don't usually take on much when I hear things, but I have some trouble I didn't want to bring up, but it's gotten bad."

"Bad how? And with the dead?" She nodded, and got up and made herself a cup of tea when his mom came in the back door. It was her turn, he knew, to watch over Rayne. "What does what Rayne can do have to do with me being the alpha, Abby?"

Making his mom a cup of tea too, she sat down and fussed with the cookies on the plate. Just when he was ready to tell her to get on with it, his mom started talking. He could only stare at her. She was making about as much sense as Abby was.

"I got the prettiest cabbage at the market today. It's the darkest shade of purple I've ever seen. I got it all the way home before I realized I haven't the slightest idea what I'm going to do with it. It would make tasty coleslaw, don't you think, Abby?" Abby nodded, but she was distracted. So was Caleb, but he wisely kept his mouth closed. "Then there were canned hams on sale. I thought about getting one of those, but then —"

"One of the kids that was bothering me, they're back. I don't know for sure if it's one of them, but they're doing the same as they'd been doing before they were caught up in that mess about eight years ago when all those boys were arrested and taken away." Caleb asked her what they were doing, still with no clue what she was talking about. "They were soaping up my windows. And stepping all over my flowers. I don't know why they're coming after me, but they are. I know it. I didn't turn them in. Mrs. Wally did."

Caleb looked at his mom for guidance. He didn't have any idea about the boys or what was going on with her house. For that matter, he didn't even remember anyone named Mrs. Wally. His mom patted him on the hand as she clarified for him.

"Mrs. Wally has passed on, son. She and her husband were setting to move to the city when she up and passed away. And he joined her a few days later. She was a nice lady…a little touched in the head about her garden, but I liked her." He asked about the boys. "They were men that were going around doing odd jobs for the pack. But one of them, and his name escapes me right now, he got it in his head to rob from them when they were inviting them in for a drink of tea or something."

"So, this one man robbed them and was run off from the pack?" Mom nodded, sipping her tea. Caleb looked over at Abby. "But he's not dead. How can you think that we can help you with him if he's not dead?"

"He is." They all turned and looked at Rayne when she entered the room, speaking. "He died about six months ago. Remorseful of his crimes. I don't think it's him."

"Then who is it?" Caleb looked from Rayne to Abby, confused. Abby got up and began fussing with the counter. There wasn't a thing wrong with it, but she scrubbed on the counters like she had found a stain that she was determined to get out. "Abby?"

Rayne sat down and put her finger to her lips. He didn't want to be hushed, he wanted answers. But when he looked at his mom for help again, she just did the same thing, like he was four years old and needed to be told to keep his tongue behind his teeth. Just as he was ready to blast Rayne, not his mom, Rayne started speaking.

"Abby, Gabe and I were wondering if you'd like to move into the house with us." Abby turned, still holding her rag like it was gold. "We have the suite done in the basement. There are even some pieces of furniture there to go with whatever you might have at your house. And that way, when the roads are bad in the winter months, you won't have to go out into the cold."

"I don't know, miss. I have no one to help me with the moving and such." When he looked at all three women, someone kicked him hard under the table. He was rubbing his battered shin when his mom cocked her brow at him.

"We could do that." Mom smiled at him. Good, he was doing something right. "The pack, we could get you packed up and moved in as soon as you want us to. And Rayne is right, you'd not have to travel in the bad weather if you stayed here."

"I don't know. What would the mister say? He might not be so keen on having an old woman staying at his house." Rayne got up and kissed Abby on the cheek. "What about them boys?"

"They're not going to bother you anymore. Why don't you go home, get your things ready to go, and then Caleb will have pack there when you're ready? And this was Gabe's idea. He knows a good thing when he sees it."

Abby left them right after that.

"I don't understand what just happened here." His mom got up and patted his cheek again. "Mom, you do know that I'm a grown man, don't you?"

"I do, but there are times when I think you'll never grow up." Mom turned to Rayne. "Thank you, my dear. I had no idea where she was going with this until you started talking. I must be off. I have a meeting in an hour with the library board. They want to cut spending, and I won't have it."

He looked at Rayne when his mom was gone too. "Can you tell me why I'm moving a very nice old lady to your sublevels? And why I just volunteered the pack to do it?"

"Yes, you're a nice man sometimes." He snorted at her. "Okay, there are no ghosts with her house. Benny, the bad boy, he's been at her home for a few weeks now, but he didn't live there with her. He wasn't hurting her or interfering with her work, but he came to me this morning and told me that she's lonely."

"And?" Caleb got up and poured himself and her a glass of tea. "She's here most of the time. There isn't any trouble at her house. I don't understand."

"She was soaping up her windows in an effort to get someone to listen to her. The smashed flowers aren't her doing, but that of a few hungry deer and raccoons that came around. The dead don't leave footprints, nor can they smash flowers. She's lonely, like I said." He still didn't understand what was going on. "Abby thought that if she got someone to think she was haunted, they'd come and live with her. Or better yet, take the time to come by and visit her daily. Working here is good for her, but she needs to be with someone. I think it's because she misses her family."

"So why didn't she just say so, instead of going around the garden twice and confusing people?" She told him he was the only one confused. "Because I would have come right out and asked."

"Yes, I can see that about you. But she's an elderly woman who needs to depend on others to help her. She doesn't have a shitload of strong brothers, parents, or a mate to keep her in line. She has, basically, only the few people that she interacts with daily that pay her." He nodded. Pride could be a good or bad thing. "So, you are getting kudos for helping her. She'll be safe in the winter months, and we have live in help when we need her. Which won't be all that necessary, but to her, it will be."

"Women are insane." She laughed and told him she was going to tell Quinn. "I'm pretty sure she'd tell you I think that because I'm an insane man. Okay, about Benny. This ghost. Is he going to be hanging around here too?"

"No, he's moved on." She drank her tea and didn't continue. Caleb didn't know why, but he was sure that she didn't know why or where he'd gone. "I have to get some work done today. My dad is dead, and I have to deal with that mess."

"If you need me, call. I'm in a helpful mood today."

Rayne looked like she was going to say more, but instead nodded once and left him there. She was out the door and her car started before he realized this wasn't his house and he was alone in it. Women were very odd.

~~~

Gabe wasn't sure he was cut out to be a country doctor. As he drove to his patient's house, he thought of all the things he'd rather be doing today, one of which was sitting with Rayne while she dealt with the aftermath of her father's death. Just as he was about to go home and call it a day instead of seeing Mrs. Patton, Rayne reached out to him.

You are not going to believe this shit. I have to figure out what to do with not just his home and properties, but also whatever else of a mess he left me. There isn't a fucking will. Did he expect to just

157

go on living forever? Or did he just, I don't know, expect to make one later? There is no later when you're a bastard like he was. He laughed, she was exactly what he needed. *I was thinking about selling this to one of your brothers. I know that Xander is the last hold out on getting himself a home. Do you think he'd take it off my hands so I don't have to mess with it? And it has this amazing studio that he can write in.*

You can ask him. I'm sure that he'd pay you fair market for it. He has the money. She said she just wanted to give it to him. *I don't know how he'd feel about that. He's been complaining a lot lately that he hasn't any idea on how much to spend on things. I think he's just waiting for someone to come along and tell him it's been a big joke, that he really doesn't have the means to sit back and write a book.*

He's no different than any of you are. You have a great deal. More now with the estate of my dad, and I'm betting you want to squirrel it away for a rainy day. You know, there aren't too many of those when it comes to living your life the way you were meant to. I don't mean just spend it willy nilly, but you need a break too. Go on a trip because you can. Have dinner at a really expensive restaurant, then tip the waiter way too much because his service was that good. Stuff. That's all, do some stuff. He did need some time away. More so in the last few weeks. *Abby is all alone because she chose to keep herself safe in her home rather than go out and live a little. It's sad really.*

Would you like to take a long trip somewhere? I don't know... our honeymoon should be spectacular. Why don't you show me Paris and other places? He was warming to the idea, and he smiled when she laughed. *The only places I've been are to college and a trip to the Bahamas when I was seventeen. Terrible experience...I'll have to tell you about it sometime.*

Deal. And while we're gone, we can shop for Christmas. It was still four months away, but he was game if she was. *I have to go now. This attorney might not make it if he doesn't stop telling me how sorry he is for my loss. So, if that happens, make sure you have enough handy to bail me out of jail. Or payoff some judge.*

He parked in front of the home of his patient, Mrs. Patton, and sat there for several minutes. Gabe was tired, that was all. It had taken a great deal out of him, worrying about Rayne when he'd converted her. He wished now that he'd been there when she woke. But he'd have the rest of his life with her, and that was good enough for him.

As soon as he entered the home, he knew there was going to be a major problem. There were perhaps a dozen ghosts in the room. Three of them were only children, but they looked to be from a different time period by the way they were dressed. Two men, wearing dark suits and ties with fedoras on their head, nodded to him, and all Gabe could think about was gangster movies. He asked no one in particular what was going on.

"She's dying."

He knew that. Mrs. Patton wasn't very old, only in her mid-sixties, but she'd been ill a great deal lately. Gabe looked at gangster number one. The woman, the living one this time, spoke again.

"All she does is complain and moan. Can you give her something that'll keep her quiet for a change?"

"They're killing her. Her grandkids. Feeding her something that ain't right. You take care of them." Gabe didn't answer the man, but he did nod slightly. "You need to take her outta here. If not, then she'll be with us sooner than she needs to be."

159

The granddaughter, Vicki, said that her grandmother had been throwing up all night. The mess was getting on her nerves. Gabe told her that it happened sometimes, and asked to see her. Alone. Vicki wasn't thrilled about that, but told Gabe she'd be close by if he needed her. He entered the room and could smell the sickness and impending death.

"Mrs. Patton?" She moaned, but didn't speak. He could see the fear in her eyes, the sadness too. "You have people here that want to help you. Do you know what Vicki is feeding you?" She looked at gangster one and he smiled at her. Family…it was certainly more extended than he had ever dreamed.

"It's over there in that toilet thing." Gabe glanced at the portable toilet and then at the man who had spoken. "I'm her nephew. I know I'm dead, you don't gotta explain things to me. But she needed me and I came running. Vicki's been feeding it to her for a few days now. I can't seem to make her stop it. I think she wants her dead for the house and stuff. Has herself all kinds of shindigs with dope and other things."

"I can take her out of here, but that won't help her when she comes back." He said he knew that, but they were aware of more things than he was. "I'm sure you do, but I'm sort of tied to the rules here. Do I call the police? Or someone else?"

"Alpha." He knew that the granddaughter was wolf, but the grandmother was human. "He can make her behave."

"Caleb can try, but it's her word against yours, and right now, I don't think that will stand up in court. Even with whatever it is in the toilet over there. Vicki could just say that she was using it for something else." He moved to the commode and lifted the lid. Inside was a half empty bottle of cleaning fluid, the strong stuff that had to be cut with water to use. "An odd place to keep cleaning things, yes, but not anything that would indicate that she was feeding it to her."

"You take her out of here. We'll deal with the girl." He wasn't sure that was right either. The rules, he had been told, were that they couldn't harm anyone that wasn't harming them. "She's my aunt. The only person in the world that loved me. I gotta help her."

"And the others? Why are they here?" Gabe looked around and realized that at some point they'd joined them in the room. "Do you all have any idea what would happen to you should you hurt that woman in the other room?"

"She's been stealing her pills. And her check." Gabe had already figured that out when Vicki had called him there to... Something occurred to him.

"Who called me? Or I mean, who of you had her call me? It doesn't seem likely that she would have done it." The young boy, one from another century, stepped forward. "You made the call?"

"I'm really old so I have some powers. I was buried out back after the sickness came to the farm. Libby, she stayed with me, feeding me broth until I was gone. I want to help her." Gabe started to explain again that he wasn't sure what removing her from the house could do to help her long term when the boy, simply called Boy, told him the rest. "That granddaughter done kilt her baby. It's under the house. If'n you go out on the back porch, I can show you. I'm betting someone like you can smell it too."

"She had a child, then killed it?" Gangster said she'd had her boyfriend help her. He took off right after. "You know his name?"

"His wallet is here." Gabe was in over his head with this.

161

He reached for his dad and mom. He told them what he knew. *And I've been told she's poisoning my patient to take over her checks and house.*

I'm with Caleb now. We'll just shimmy on over there for a looksee. Gabe told him about the cleaning stuff, as well as the ghosts in the room with him. *You keep them safe. I don't know how you'd go about that, but we're on our way. And Caleb is calling the police now.*

He told them what was going on, and was just examining Mrs. Patton when Vicki joined him in the room. Gabe wanted to ask her why she'd hurt her own grandmother, but decided he might be tipping his hand. Instead, he asked if she had noticed anything more about her symptoms.

"She whines a great deal. Gets on my nerves with it. I know that I shouldn't do it, but I shut her up in here when it gets to be too much." He asked about her medications. "Oh, yeah. She dumped them out the other morning. I had to scrape up enough for her to have her shit for today. You'll have to write her another one, I'm guessing. And could you make it for like three months at a time? It's hard for me to find someone to sit with her while I go get it every month."

"I'll see about having them brought out here daily, with a nurse to administer them to her." She said that wouldn't do for her. "I'm not concerned with you, Vicki, but for your grandmother. She's very ill and the medications are to keep her alive. The county can do this for her at no charge. I insist."

"I don't want nobody in my house that I don't know." Gabe nearly pointed out that it wasn't her house but her grandmother's when he heard someone pull in the drive. "Who the hell could that be? Damn it all to fuck and back. You don't do nothing to her until I come back here. She needs

162

me to take care of her, and I will."

While Vicki was at the door, he pulled out his cell phone. Just as he was calling for an ambulance to take Mrs. Patton to the hospital to take care of her, a big man came in the room with them. He looked pissed off.

"This is the boyfriend. The one I was telling you about." He nodded at Boy. "He means to hurt you. If'n I was you, I'd skedaddle on out of here. Unless'n you've called in some help."

Instead of running, which he did want to do in the worst kind of way, he smiled at Burly, even going so far as to putting out his hand in friendship. It was slapped away, as if Gabe had insulted him at some point. The low growl didn't make his wolf any happier than he was. The kid had to know that he was brother to the alpha.

"Hello. I was just telling Vicki here that I can have someone come out and help with the burden of taking care of her grandmother." Burly said she wasn't going nowhere. "Well, I don't think that's for you to decide. I'm her physician, and I say it's necessary."

"Like I said, you ain't taking the breadwinner out of here. We got us some plans, and that don't work if you take her out where she can't help us out." Gabe asked him how she helped. "Checks. Them drugs. Did Vicki tell you that we needed more of them? I got some guy lined up to buy all we can get him. And if you keep writing them scripts, we can cut you in on the deal."

"I don't think so. And Vicki said that she spilled her medications. Now you're telling me that you're selling them? You do know that's against the law, don't you?" Burly, or whatever his name really was, just smiled. He had five gold

163

teeth, and three so badly rotted that they looked like they belonged on some creature from a horror film. "You know, for the money that you spend on those gold capped teeth, you could have gotten your whole mouth cleaned up. I'm sure that Vicki doesn't mind, but those are fucking nasty. And could be what makes you think you can scare me with these big man tactics."

As soon as Burly lunged at him, shifting as he did so, he was caught up by the scruff of his neck by Caleb. The man's wolf was as nasty as his mouth, dirty and unkempt. After a hard shake, his brother tossed him against the wall. Burly didn't move, which was a good thing because Caleb looked ready to cause him some serious harm. Instead, Burly seemed like he was submitting. But from the expression on Caleb's face, it was much too late for that.

"I had this, you know?" Caleb said he was sure that he did, but he didn't want him to have all the fun. "All I got to do was make fun of him. I'm sure that what you did was much better."

"I'm sorry. The next time a lunatic comes after you, I'll stand back and let you get your ass handed to you. It'll be my pleasure, as a matter of fact." He called him a jackass, which earned him a slap on the back from his dad. "What else is going on here? I'm assuming that you had help?"

"Yes."

Vicki came in at that moment and rushed to Burly. As soon as she turned on him, Caleb stepped in front of Gabe and told her to heel. She didn't, and that didn't go over well at all.

Chapter 12

The house was cold. Not just because of the chill in the air, but the structure itself. She hadn't enjoyed her childhood there, and now that she was an adult, she hated the place even more. Nothing inside made her think that she could have ever been happy there, if she'd had any plans of living there. And she was going to be glad to get rid of it.

The chill in the room grew slightly colder, and she looked around. Without her mom around, Rayne was a little nervous. When she saw him, standing just inside the room she was in, Rayne went back to work, ignoring her father.

"So, you've finally gotten what you've always wanted." Rayne looked at her father, but said nothing to him. "I'm going to blame all this on you, should anyone ask me. You caused my death by being born."

"If you say so." She continued to look through the papers on the desk. "Was there ever a time that you had enough money and power? Just looking at these accounts, I can see that you were very wealthy, yet you continued to try for

165

more. Was there a reason for it? Did you think you had some special powers that would allow you to take it with you? In the event you didn't know, you don't have any use for money where you are."

"Money is what makes a person more powerful. It matters little where you find yourself. And since you killed me by being a malicious child, I think that you'll soon be joining me here. Just look at that moron you're thinking of marrying. He has money out the ass, and yet he goes to work every day like he enjoys being at people's beck and call. I'm guessing that you don't have any use for this money now that you have him." She told him what her plans were. "Yes, yes. You said that before. A woman's shelter. What for? Do you think that some women don't care for being knocked around a bit?"

"I'm sure that most don't. But it's not just a woman's shelter, but a shelter for all people. Children included, in this case. There are some abused men, you know." He called them pussies. "To you, perhaps. But, as you might have guessed, I don't care what you think."

"Rayne McFarland, the misunderstood child of the ball breaking Carson McFarland. Quite a legacy that you have going for you. Are you going to carry on my name? Bring some little fuckers into your life that will turn out just like their old grandda? That would be just perfect if you asked me." Rayne started making piles of things that she needed to take care of. Mostly it was unpaid bills for the house. Insurance due on the car. "I'm speaking to you, young lady. You can at least show me that you are slightly heartbroken that I'm dead."

"I'm not heartbroken at all. In fact, I'm quite relieved that you're gone. One less thing that I have to worry over. You can't be trying to kill me anymore while you're there.

Why didn't you pay the car insurance for the year and save some money? I would have thought that would have been something that you would have jumped right onto." Rayne ignored his ranting about how she wasn't a good daughter, as well as a few other choice things she was terrible at. "I'm going to sell this house, and the contents, for a buck. Though why anyone would want the shit you have in here is beyond me."

"You will do no such thing. This is my house and I've put a lot of hard work into it. You'll put it on the market for what it's worth, not some low amount like that to get back at me. I had this house appraised not long ago, and it was valued in the millions. So help me, Rayne, you do this and I will never forgive you." She didn't even bother with a reply. "This is my legacy to people who respected me. I had to show them what a big man I was, how the rich lived and that they'd never be able to be like me. All this money and homes, it was necessary to make me powerful. You should have more respect for what I've done, and not be stupid with it by selling it off to some white trash that will make a mess here within seconds of moving in."

"Should they have respect for you? When you did nothing at all for them, including not stealing from them or having them killed? Well, that's not going to happen. I have a bill here for three suits that you ordered. Did you pick them up? I don't want to have to pay for them if you didn't get them yet. Perhaps I'll have you buried in one of them." He told her she was ungrateful. "Maybe, but you're a prick and a murderer, so I think in the long run, I'm much better. Did you pick up the suits or not?"

"Get away from my things." Rayne pointed out that they

167

were hers now. "I didn't give you anything. You can't even find where I left a will because I didn't have one. Who would have thought that I'd be dead at such a young age?"

"Doesn't matter. I'm your daughter, the only living relative that you didn't manage to murder, so it's all mine. And thinking that you weren't going to catch a bullet at any age is stupid on your part. You should have been killed before you murdered my mother." He pointed out that she might not have been here if that would have happened. "Or, more than likely I would have still been born, and you wouldn't have been my father. I like that scenario better."

She knew that she was pissing him off, but it didn't matter to her. She knew that she was much stronger than he'd ever been, and if he fucked with her, he would be banished from her life. Rayne was going to keep him from the house, just for the next person who lived here. And without him hanging around, she thought she might be able to move on quicker, getting on with her own life without worrying about him being over her shoulder all the time.

"There are things in that safe that I want you to bury with me. Notes and such. For men that I have promised to keep safe no matter what happened to me." Rayne looked at the large picture on the wall and knew that was where the safe was. "You don't need to know what's in there. Have someone that I trust to open it for you."

"Or, here is what I'm thinking...I'll open it, since you were stupid enough to have left the combination out where I could find it, and I'll take care that the men on your lists are taken to jail. Why should you have all the say in any of this?" Her father came to the safe just as she was getting up to open it. "You don't really think you can take me on, do you? Do you have any idea who I am?"

"Yes, I was told. Some people even said that I should be proud of you. Like that is ever going to happen. You're nothing to me. Never have been, and now that I'm dead, you won't be either." Just as she had thought, but it was still painful to hear it from his lips. "I want you out of here. Now. I have no need for you to clean up after me. That's what I pay the attorneys for."

"Too bad." She put the code in to open the safe. Rayne was a little afraid to do this…there was no telling what she might find in here. But when he told her again to get away, she pulled the door open and stood looking at the contents.

Sitting on the floor, she didn't know what to do. There were papers inside, a great many of them that she'd have to go over, but it was the stacks of money. Just from her position on the floor, she counted fifty of them. Looking at her father, she asked him what he'd done this for.

"My running money. Fat lot of good it did me. Andrew came in here and shot me like I meant nothing to him." She told him that he'd had his son killed. "So? I tried to have you killed too, yet here you are. He should have known this was coming. His son was a dick. I would have thought that he'd think I was doing him a favor. It would have been to me, should someone had killed you off before this."

"Yet it was your plan for me to marry him. For what?" He told her what his plan was. "I see, and that didn't do you a lot of good either, did it? I had the money, you didn't know where it was, and I'm happy." Rayne laughed. "That must be the worst part for you, that I'm happy."

"He would have kept you in line. And after a while, you would have met with an unfortunate accident like your mother

169

did. But he would have made out with that too. Insurance money can be had for all sorts of cash. Easy money, I call it." She started pulling out the things in the safe. "What do you think you're doing? I told you that it didn't belong to you."

"You're right, it belongs to the people who you destroyed." She was just finishing up logging things into her book when Sara showed up. Rayne told her what her plans for the money were. "Do you think this is a good idea? To open up a retirement home for some of the elderly?"

"We used to have one here, many years ago now. I don't think it was run by the most trustworthy of people. There was some talk about some of the residents being hurt too, but nothing could be proven so it shut down." Rayne knew nothing about running a place like that and told her so. "Neither do I, but I'm betting that with our resources we can find someone that does. And I've been reading this lovely article about how some of the grade schoolers go to nursing homes and talk to the elderly. It's working out well for all of them."

"I think that is a great idea." She looked at her father who had been screaming at her to shut her mouth for the last ten minutes. "I'm going to give this house to Xander. Perhaps he can find himself a story or two in it. I'm sure there are a few here."

"Oh, lovely. If you don't mind, I'll butter him up for you about it. There is something about this place that creeps me out a bit, but you can more than likely take care of that, can't you?" Rayne smiled at her. "If it's your father, dear, I'd just send him on his way. There is no point in him being here when he was nothing more than a cruel reminder of what he did to your mother. Such a nasty man to have sired such a lovely daughter. The man should have been shot years ago."

"He murdered my mom. Planned my death as well. I don't want to banish him to the unliving, but I don't think he'll be any better to have around than Blaine is." Sara asked where he was. "I'm sure that he won't be far. He has it in his head that I can bring him back to life. I can't, Father, if that is what you were going to say."

"You should be able to do whatever I tell you. I'm your father, after all." Rayne laughed as she told Sara what he'd said. "I do not think this is a funny situation, Rayne. You are to leave my house just the way you found it. My attorney knows just how to take care of things."

"I'm sure that he does, but I'm in charge now, not you." She stood up, hugging Sara when she came to help. "My mom left me. She said that her work here was finished here with me, and that I had someone to keep me safe. She didn't say it, but I don't think she was just talking about Gabe, but all of you."

"What a nice thing to say to me. Yes, we'll keep you safe. And you'll go on fixing things for the unliving for us. I'm sure that we'll be all right from now on. And this house? I think that Xander will love it here." They started for the door to the hall and she turned back to her father. "Get rid of the trash, dear. You'll feel much better if you do."

"Rayne, don't you dare." She smiled at her father and raised her hand up. It wasn't anything she needed to do, but it did shut him up.

"You are no longer welcome in my life, nor in my family's lives, in my homes, or the homes of any member of my family. You will be banished if you come near us and let yourself be known." He opened his mouth and she cut him off. "Be gone."

Rayne knew that it was painful for the dead to be sent away from an area. Not just physically, she'd been told, but mentally too. Once, long ago, she'd sent a man from his family because he'd been harming them by hauntings. Her mom told her later that she'd seen the man later, and that he was broken, and couldn't remember anything. Rayne had finally banished him just to give him a little peace. Or her some. She was never sure which.

Walking the rest of the house with Sara, it was quiet, just as she thought it would be from now on. Entering the room that she had thought of for Xander, she paused in the doorway. There was no one there, but she could feel them. She asked Sara to wait.

"No, I don't think I will. You might be harmed, and I'd never forgive myself." She told her that she'd rather be hurt than her. "Then I guess we go in together. What is it you feel?"

"Someone." As she moved into the room, she looked around. There weren't any places that a ghost could hide, but she did what she normally did when she wasn't sure who was there. "Come out or be gone."

The child moved out of the bottom shelf of the tall bookshelf that had a door on it. The space was to hold any manner of things, she supposed, but it was cleaned out, containing only a small pillow and blanket. It took her several moments to realize that it was a child, and not the ghost of one. She stood there staring at them both, she and Sara, like she had no idea where she was or what she was doing there.

"My name is Rayne. My father used to own this house." The girl said nothing. Rayne thought she might be as old as ten, but not much more than that. "This is Sara Winchester. Her son is my future husband."

"The doctor." Rayne told her that was right and moved into the room more. "Don't. I don't want you to come any closer, please. There are things here, people you can't see."

"Yes, I know. Can you see them too?" She nodded and looked in the corner. Then Rayne saw her. "Do you know who that is?"

"My mom. She and I were hurt by Mr. McFarland. He wasn't a nice man." She told her that she didn't think so either. "Mom died about a year ago. I've been here since. In the middle of the night, I go and eat. I haven't taken anything more than some food."

"It's all right. You take whatever you need. Mr. McFarland is dead, did you know that?" She told her that she was there when it happened. "I'm sorry about that. Did he know you were here?"

"No, I don't think he would have allowed me to stay if he had known." Rayne watched as her mom moved toward the little girl. "She watched out for me when he was here. Not so much anymore, but I think that's why I could live here. How is it you can see her?"

"I see them all." The girl looked at her mom, who told her who she was. "I was wondering if you're hungry? I mean, Sara and I were about to go get some dinner, and we'd love for the two of you to come with us."

"She can't leave here." Rayne asked her where her body was. "In the basement. She's under the new pool table down there. How did you know she was buried here?"

"He wouldn't have wanted her found, I think, and he would have also wanted her close by to remind himself of his power. I can get her some help, if you'd like. She would be able to move on. I'm sorry, I don't know your name." She told her who she was. "All right, Penny. We can take care of your mom when we come back, or we can order pizza for here. What would you like to do?"

"Order." Rayne asked Sara to take her to the kitchen to find a phone. They both had cell phones on them, but she wanted to talk to the woman alone. "I've never had pizza at a house before. Is it really good?"

They wandered off, their voices getting lower the further they went into the house. Rayne looked at the ghost and could see the ravages that had been put upon her body. She'd been beaten severely before her death.

"I'd like for her to go out, miss. She's been stuck here for too long now." Rayne asked her what her name was. "Sharon Wiseman. My daughter is eleven, but she will need someone to care for her if you sell off the house."

"I can take you out without someone finding you, Sharon. But you won't be able to stay with your daughter if I do." Sharon nodded. "You could live here, if you wish. I can make sure that the man I'm going to sell the house to is aware that you're here. And then Penny can come and see you."

"You'd do that?" Rayne said it would be her pleasure. "I don't want to be found. I don't want to put Penny through anything more. She's had it hard, what with the mister knocking her around like he did me. He thought she was dead, I think."

"More than likely." She didn't know what to do with the child, but she had to do something. "Sharon, is there anyone that I can notify about Penny? Someone to take her into their home?"

"No one. Her dad is dead…not by this man, but an accident. It's why I came here to work. My parents are both gone and his mom is in a nursing home. I don't have anyone to keep her safe." Rayne told her that she would come to live with them. "Oh, no, I can't ask you to do that, miss. She's a little girl that has no relationship to you."

"It doesn't matter. She's going to need some help with seeing the dead. You know that as well as I do. They'll take her to task a lot more than she can handle if she's not careful." Sharon said that a couple had already. "I'll take her to my home, and it's not that far for her to come here. And I'll bring her, no matter the time, so that she can visit you. Will that be all right?"

"Yes, I couldn't have imagined you doing this for us. She's all I have." Rayne knew that feeling more than anyone. "Thank you so much. I can't remember when anyone has ever been this nice to me before. I mean, since my husband died. Thank you again."

"It's all right. I'll help her and she'll do all right in the end. But you know the rules." Sharon nodded. "Good. I don't want anything to happen to either of you. Just do what is right by her and we'll all get along."

"Yes, I promise. I know I keep saying this, but thank you so much."

Rayne joined them in the kitchen a few minutes later. She was happy to see that Penny and Sara seemed to be getting along so well, and worried about the impact on their lives when Penny came to stay with them.

"I have to talk to Gabe." Sara smiled at her. "You told him, didn't you? And I suppose you asked Xander to come over here too. What am I going to do with you?"

"Love me, I hope. And yes, to both questions. I knew that you'd get around to telling Gabe sooner or later, but I told

175

him now so that you could deal with the things left undone here."

Going to the back door when someone knocked on it, she wasn't the least bit surprised to find the delivery guy there with nine large pizzas. Rayne looked at Sara and asked her who she thought was going to eat all that. "In the event that you've not figured it out, the family is coming here. They're excited to meet the newest member of the family."

Taking both Xander and Gabe around the house, she realized that she didn't know this place. She'd been here when she was a child, of course, but it looked as if all traces of her were gone. Even her old room was nothing but a bedroom without any feeling in it. She didn't hate this house, she just didn't know it.

"The little girl, you said that her mom was here. Buried in the basement." Rayne told Xander she didn't want to be disturbed. "I can understand her reasoning as well. To put her daughter through that would be hard. I'd like for her to live here with me."

"You don't have to do that, Xander. We can raise her." Xander nodded, but moved into the hall away from them. Rayne looked at Gabe. "You don't mind raising her, do you? I mean, she's had a hard life."

"She has. And when I told Xander about her life, he told me that it's unfair to uproot her. He really wants to do this." Rayne asked him what he thought. "I think that she could help Xander. The house is certainly big enough for the two of them to live here. And he's already talking about live in help as well for them. I think, to him, this is a done deal. He will be a good father to her."

Of that, Rayne had no doubt. Xander was so quiet; his life

seemed to be organized to the point where it was painful for him at times. But she could also see him being a good father figure to Penny...plus, she'd be close to her mom. It was a win-win for them both.

"Carmen is going to take care of the paperwork for them. I know that it seems rushed to you, but actually, I think he's been looking for something to devote himself to for a while now. And when I mentioned that there was a child, he said he'd take her." Rayne asked Gabe why this one. "I don't know, love. Perhaps this is in the same manner as us finding our mates. This child was destined to be his no matter what."

"But not his mate." Gabe said no, not his mate, but he'd love her like his own. "I don't have a problem with any of this, but I can worry. She's just a little girl, and he's a single man. What can they have in common that will help them?"

"Life." She didn't like the answer, but it was a good one. "She'll be safe and taken care of. He'll have someone to roam this house with. And once the paperwork goes through, Xander will have a little girl to brighten all our lives."

Within hours, not only had she sold the house to Xander for a buck, but he had signed the paperwork that would change all their lives forever. Penny Winchester seemed to be overwhelmed but happy. Xander was moving things from his parents' house into the big mansion with the help of family.

Rayne had all the money removed from the safe, as well as any paperwork that she could find. A cleaning crew was coming in the morning to take out the suits and any of the other personal items of her father's. Xander could keep or toss out anything that he didn't want, but he seemed satisfied with what was there. Rayne couldn't be happier for him. Things were turning out right for a change.

177

Chapter 13

Nothing. Not a single bank robbery. The money was real, and the bank was only amazed at the shape that the hundred and fifty-year-old bill was in. The manager, a good friend of Owen's, even called someone to see if the money had been part of a robbery that hadn't been reported, and found nothing on it. Owen had no idea what he was supposed to do now. Not having anywhere else to turn, he reached out to his brothers.

I need you to come over to my house. Now, if you can. Caleb asked him what was going on. *I found something. A lot of somethings in my barn. I need your help and advice on it. It's not terrible, but...Just come over, please.*

They were there in an hour. Even his dad showed up, telling him that he'd been with Dominic when the call had come in. Owen had brought all the trunks to the house, even the ones that he'd yet to open, and took his family to the living room. He told them what he'd been doing when he came across them.

"I actually thought about making the barn into a studio.

179

I'm not talented enough to think that I'd be able to make a living at it, but I enjoy painting. So, I thought that it would be a good place to enjoy it without smelling up the house. But there was—"

"You're taking too long. Get to the point." He growled low at Tyler. "Well, you are. What's up? We can figure this out if you give us a clue as to what you've found."

Instead of answering him, he went to the first trunk and opened it. This one was filled with the tea cups. When they looked them over, marveling as he had at how beautiful and well preserved they were, he walked to the one with the watches in it.

"If I didn't know better, I would have thought this was from Mr. Cartwright. But some of these are very expensive. Even back when they were made." His dad picked up the watch that Owen had fallen in love with and held it to the light. "That one is worth more than any of the ones that I got from Mr. Cartwright. It's handmade and nearly two hundred years old. And still works."

"You have a fortune here." Owen told Gabe that wasn't all. "What is it? You find a trunk of money?"

"Yes." No one moved or spoke. Opening the next trunk, the one that he'd been terrified of being stolen since he found it, he stood over it while telling them what he'd figured out. "The money has no ill will attached to it. There are no robberies reported, or at least not in the papers. No claims on it that we can find, and it's all real. Every dollar of it."

"How much?" He told Dominic. "You just found this? In the barn? What the hell was it doing out there? You think the previous owners did it?"

"I had my attorney contact them and ask about the

contents of the barn and other sheds on the property. They told him, and put it in writing, that it was mine, they had no holds over any of it. I didn't tell him what I'd found, only that I wanted to make sure that it was mine to do with as I wanted. It is. All of it." They sat down, every one of them, as if their knees would no longer hold them. "There are five more trunks that I'm terrified to open, if you want to know the truth. For all I know there could be a dead body in them that has been preserved with the cash. I'm in over my head here, and I don't know what the fuck to do about it."

"You don't put it in the bank, that's for sure. I mean, I don't want to break the law in this, but can you imagine what sort of trouble you could get into with this type of find? They'd be all over you in a heartbeat." His dad picked up one of the stacks and then put it back before continuing. "And the amount of people coming out of the woodwork claiming that it belonged to them would be just terrible. By the time the dust settled, you'd be lucky if you got to keep the trunks."

That was what Owen had thought as well, and was glad that someone else had thought of it. But still, he didn't have any idea how to keep the money and not be in trouble too. He looked at Dominic when he cleared his throat.

"When you found the money, what was the first thing you thought of after the shock?" He told him. "Okay, other than putting it in the bank, which you have to agree isn't the best idea, then what?"

"I really thought of some of the things going on within our family. The businesses that are going in downtown. The shelter for the abused. I even thought of the school where you work, as well as the campgrounds. Horses. I have no idea why, but I thought of horses like we used to have when we were kids. A lot of just random things." He looked at Gabe. "What can you see here? I mean, is there someone just, I don't know, hanging around waiting to have me murdered in my sleep for disturbing their little stash?"

"You do have a very vivid imagination, don't you? Are you watching those crime shows again? Don't. They're messing with your head." Gabe asked to go out to the barn with him. "That way, if there is someone out there, we can ask them about it. But as far as the house, there isn't anyone here that might have known or they'd be in the room with us."

Owen was nearly to the barn when he realized what his brother had said. No one in the house was in the room with them. Did that mean there was someone in the house? Or a lot of someones? He decided, for now at least, he'd not ask him. But taking him to the barn, he was worried at what they might find out there.

The climb up the ladder was easier than it had been coming down last night. The trunks were heavy, yes, but they were also scary large. He'd been up and down the rungs so much that he felt in pretty good shape. But when Gabe paused at the top without going the rest of the way, he almost started down them again.

"You see anyone?" Gabe just looked down at him from his lofty perch. "Don't tell me. I've decided just now to put all the money and trunks back in here and forget about them. It's fine, tell the person I don't need it."

"It's a family. They've been waiting on you to return." Gabe went the rest of the way up and disappeared. Owen didn't move. He wasn't sure that he could. When he saw Gabe again, peering down at him, he told him he was going home. "Get up here, dumbass. I was joking with you."

Owen was going to throw his brother over the loft. It was a good plan until he remembered that he'd more than likely haunt him for the rest of his life. Stomping up the ladder, he walked to where Gabe was crouched down and saw something that he'd not seen before.

"What is that? A diary?" Gabe told him that's what it looked like to him. "Damn it, it's going to have a will in it, I know it. And I'm going to have to find this long-lost person and—"

"What is wrong with you? Christ, are you taking notes on this shit that is spewing from your mouth? Maybe you could give them to Xander and he could write a best seller with them. Just take a deep breath, let it out, and then take the fucking book. You're making me insane." Owen really was contemplating how hard it would be to murder his brother when he picked up the book on his own. "Let's go in the house. See what this says and work from there. If there were people here, they aren't now. I'll talk to Rayne. Maybe she can figure out if anyone was ever here."

When he got back to the house, he was glad to see that someone had opened the last of the trunks. It was more of the same thing. No more cash, thankfully, but there were photographs, as well as some small handpainted pictures in two of them.

One entire trunk was devoted to art supplies, most of them still in their original boxes and cartons. A few rolls of canvas had yellowed a little, and paintbrushes, hundreds of them, were in varying shapes and sizes.

"I've seen this name before. I don't remember where, but I've seen some of this person's work." Xander went to the computer and asked for the spelling of the name again. Once he had it, he laughed. "I knew that I had. I mean, this has to be the same person. Birdie J. Felton died some years ago. She had some pretty profitable shows when she was alive."

"When did she pass away?" Xander told him she'd been dead since nineteen eighty-six and was a hundred and two years old. "Wow, that's a very long time. And these things, you think they belonged to her? That some of this might be hers?"

"This article says that she died alone. No children from her one and only marriage. That she was worth millions when she died, but no one had ever seen the money. The bank that she dealt with at the time claims that she would come in occasionally, cash her checks she'd get, and take the money with her. So, yes, that's what I would assume as well. Christ, this is amazing." Xander was quiet for several moments. "You're going to love this part. She collected tea cups wherever she went, as well as men's watches. It says here that she was obsessed with them. That before she could sign on at a place for a show, there had to be a little men's shop close to where she'd be staying."

There was talk about the things in the other trunks. More watches were in one, as well as a lot of art supplies. Some tea cups as well. There was even an order for a set of them with monthly designs that were to be shipped to her. Owen wondered if she ever got them, and where the rest of her cups were.

When his family left, he went to the computer to look up what else he could find about the woman. At four in the morning, he found something that wasn't widely known, he'd bet. There had been a child born of the woman, a boy, and it had occurred before she had found her husband. She was young, only sixteen, when he'd been born, and it hinted that the child had died. But the more he read about her, he came to realize that not only did the child not die, but that she sent money to someone named Macintosh twice a month.

That search was going to have to wait until the morning, he decided, and made his way to his room. But not before sending a message to his attorney for him to find out all he could about the child, Michael Macintosh. Giving him all he could figure out — birthday, state of birth, as well as who might have adopted him — was his only hope of figuring out who this person might be.

~~~

"Conrad, there's a call for you." He made his way to the phone and picked it up. Saying his name, he heard someone talking and waited. Conrad still had a lot of dishes to wash up before he could go home, and he didn't want to be in trouble for not getting it done on time.

"Mr. Macintosh?" He told the caller that his name was Conrad. "All right. My name is Gilbert Wayne. I was wondering if we could sit down and talk sometime soon. Whenever it's convenient for you."

He knew better than to agree to anything. Conrad might be stupid, but he knew that people would take advantage of him when they could. Looking at the stacks of dishes he had to wash, he told the man that he didn't have any time.

"It's important that I speak to you. And soon. There have been some inquiries about your grandparents." He told him they were both dead. "Yes, I'm aware of that. It's why I'm calling to speak to you."

"I can't talk to you." He started to hang up the phone when the man began talking again. He politely waited for him to be done. "I'm not allowed to talk to you. I have to wait until someone helps me."

"You have help?" He said that he did. "You can bring them along with you, if you want. I just need to ask you a few questions that this person is asking me. It won't take long."

"I'll figure it out. You can call me here tomorrow and I'll let you know." He didn't wait for the man to reply, but hung up the phone. Before he could forget, he wrote down the man's name, Gilbert Wayne, with the help of one of the waitresses where he worked. Then he went back to his dishes.

Conrad took great pride in having a job that paid him. He'd been working in the school lunchroom where he had been staying until about six months ago. It was then that his little sister came to get him to have him live with her. She was good to him too. Never yelled or made him feel bad about how dumb he was. Which he had to remember not to call himself when she was around.

Smiling, he thought of his sister, Clare. She sure could get up in your business if she thought you were doing something bad. Like him calling himself a retard. She'd been so mad that someone had called him that, that Conrad had never told her that everyone did and he was all right with it. He sure didn't want her to go to the big jail because she killed everybody.

Conrad knew that he'd been put away when he'd hurt her a long time ago. He'd not meant to, but she was so tiny that he'd squeezed her too tight and had made her cry. Right after that he'd been taken to the home for dummies, another thing he wasn't supposed to say, and his mom and dad said he was going to die there. He about did…his heart had been broken because Mom and Dad had taken Clare away from him.

When she'd come for him, he'd been so shocked that he didn't know her. Clare had grown up to be so pretty, and her hair was all shiny too. Touching his fingers gently to her face, he'd smiled when she did.

"I missed you." He nodded, tears filling his eyes. "I've got a good job now, and I can afford to care for us both."

"Mom and Dad, they told me I have to die here because I hurt you." She hugged him again and told him that they were both gone. It took him a whole month to understand that they were both dead. He'd been so terrified they'd come back and take him to the place again.

He was better now, and taking some classes at the college that he enjoyed. Things like writing a check and using the computer better. And he was drawing again. They would take his paper and pens from him when he lived in the home, but Clare, she gave him money all the time for chores that he'd do and he would buy his own things. And for his birthday last month, she'd gotten him some pretty paints and some canvas. He was in pickle heaven now.

After his shift was over, the waitress, Betty, she gave him the paper with the name on it. His writing wasn't too good, but he knew that Clare would be able to read it. She called it his special language, and that made her laugh. Walking home, he thought of what he wanted to paint first, and decided that he needed to bring his camera with him so he could take some pictures. Then he remembered his new cell phone.

Taking pictures with it wasn't easy for him. He knew that he had to push the little camera to get it to come up, but he kept forgetting to not touch the little circle in the middle first. Conrad got four pictures that he thought were going to be good, and more than that of things like his fingers, he was

187

sure. Once he got home, he knew that Clare would help him print them off.

The house was locked up when he got home, but he had a key. It was a rare treat for him to beat his sister home from work, and he went to the kitchen to fix them both a salad. He loved fresh salad, and Clare liked tomatoes. Careful not to cut himself, Conrad got all the things in a bowl just as she got home.

"What a day. Did you have a good day at work, Conrad?" He told her about the call. He had to do that first thing or he'd forget. "What did he want?"

"He said he wanted to sit down and talk to me and you. I told him that I wasn't allowed to talk to him without help, and he said I could bring you too." She said that she'd go with him, just to set it up in the evenings.

That was another thing he loved about Clare...she didn't just take over his things like regular people did. When he was doing something, she'd only come help him if he asked or she thought he was going to get hurt. He'd done that a few times as well.

The salad was really good when she cut up some chicken to go over it. His favorite thing to eat with salad was everything. Grinning, he told her what he wanted for dinner tomorrow night.

"I can get a roast on the way home from the studio, but we won't be able to have it tomorrow night. How about we have that on Thursday, and I'll even make some homemade noodles to go with it?" He thought that was a super idea. "You can make us another salad. And maybe, if I can clean up on time, I can pick us up a pineapple pie."

"I like pie." Clare smiled at him. "I'm going to paint for a little while. Then we can watch television. Okay?"

"Yes. All right. I'll clean up since you did most of the work." He loved Clare and told her that. "I love you too, Conrad. With all my heart."

Printing out the pictures, he laughed when she did at the shots of his fingers he'd gotten. There weren't that many, but he did manage to get a couple of his shoes too. She told him he'd be better at it someday, and he thought she was right.

When he was going to his room, she gave him a small box. In it was the camera he'd had when he lived with her when she was a baby. Living at his mom and dad's with her had been special to him.

"I found it in some of the things I got from the house. I had it cleaned up for you, and there is film in it. When you have it done, give it to me and I'll take it in to be developed for you. Or you can. I think it's on the way home from your work." He said she could do it the first time, but he'd go with her. "All right. That way I can set you up with an account."

Conrad loved to paint. He wasn't as good as Clare was — she was super good — but he was having fun. And that, she told him, was the most important thing. As he carefully put some of the paint on his pallet, he didn't take his eyes off the task. He'd made a mess once, and while Clare didn't get mad at him, he knew that he'd done a bad thing. So now he was very careful.

The picture that he was going to paint was of a dandelion. He liked the way the only one that was yellow was in the center of the bunch. The rest of them had gone to seed. The green grasses with the few fall leaves were pretty too, and he was excited to get it going. As soon as he had the colors he wanted to start with poured, he sat down to the canvas and let out a long breath.

He'd done that since he'd been given a brush by his grandda. He'd been a painter too, and his daddy had been one as well. As far as he knew, Conrad's dad had never picked up a brush. Not even to paint the house when it was needed. But Clare and he, they both loved to paint, and that was what Clare said put food on their tables. He loved how she made things all easy for him to remember.

When she came into his little room that he used for painting, he showed her what he'd done. As she looked it over, never saying anything at first, he looked at it too. The flower was there but not done, and he was really happy with the way that the dandelions that were all dried up looked. She asked him what he was going to name it.

"I was thinking on that when I took the picture." Clare sat on his other chair and waited on him to tell her. "You're going to think it's dumb."

"No I won't. You want to know why?" He nodded. "The painting that I started today, I'm calling it Rushing Seasons. There is a tree on one side of the painting that is in full fall colors, while the one right next to it is still in summer. I think that sounds like a television series rather than a painting."

"You're so funny. I'm going to call it Sprout. Like the seeds will sprout out and make more flowers for me to paint." She looked at the picture again, then at him. "You don't like it. I'll think of something—"

"No, you will not. I like it. It's a good title for it. Sprout. Yes, it's perfect. People will wonder about the title, think of their own versions as to why an artist would paint it and name it that. You did well, Conrad. Very well."

When she left him to go to bed—it was much later than

he thought it was — he looked at his painting. He thought he'd done well. The grass was as green as he could make it, and the yellow was the perfect shade of the picture. As he was cleaning up his mess, he thought of the title again. Yes, he thought, it was perfect.

Conrad went to his bedroom smiling. He was a free man, his sister told him, and he loved it. Conrad couldn't wait to go to the auction house with her on Saturday of next week. They were going to have some fun.

Chapter 14

Gabe was down to his last half hour when the door opened to the front offices. He got up, having already told Martha that she could go home. He saw Rayne there, her face bloodied and her lip swollen. Going to her, he pulled her into one of his rooms, asking her who had done this to her.

"No one." He just stared at her. "Really. No one did this. I was coming off the ladder at the house when I slipped down to the floor. And since I had my hands full, the stuff hit me in the face. I drove myself here because Abby was freaking out a bit."

"What the hell were you doing on the ladder anyway?" He cleaned her face up and then made sure that she wasn't going to need stitches. "You do know that you could shift and this would be all gone."

"I'm not ready for that yet." He nodded. "Besides, I think that would have sent Abby into hysterics. The woman has it in her head that you need to be with me the first time I do that." He wanted to be there too.

193

"Look, it's not that bad, really. How about you hang around here, and when I'm done and all locked up, we'll go home and you can shift?" She smiled at him, and he felt as if he could conquer the world. "I only have to stay for twenty more minutes."

"You're the boss, you know that, right?" He kissed her on the nose and went to lock up. "I drove in, so I'll go ahead and leave and you can come after you're done."

"Nope. We're going to go together. We'll come back tomorrow for the car." He didn't want her to change her mind, or heaven forbid someone to come to them that needed help. He was needy enough. "Okay, just wait here and I'll take us home."

Gabe hated locking up early, even if it was only a few minutes. But for the past hour, he'd been done with appointments and had been playing on his computer to fill the time. Turning the lock, he headed back to the room he'd left Rayne in, and nearly fell back when she was lying on the table, naked.

"I was wondering if you could do a very thorough examination on me. You know, make sure that I didn't hurt anything else when I fell. I could have some major damage to myself and you might have missed it." He nodded, but didn't move. "I think you'd have to be a little closer to make sure."

"You're naked." She nodded and smiled at him. "I really should make sure. I mean, as my mate, I don't want anything to be coming up later."

"Yes, I agree. And so that I'm not too uncomfortable being naked, I think you should be too." He took off his lab coat and dropped it to the floor. "Come here, Gabriel. I want to make sure that you don't miss any of your clothing."

She got up from the table, and he had to swallow twice before he could speak. Then it only came out as gibberish, so he shut up. As his belt left the loops on his pants, his cock stretched, thickening in anticipation of taking her. But then she dropped to her knees in front of him and put her hands on his thighs.

"I thought I was going to make sure you were all right." She grinned as she unsnapped the snap at his pants. The zipper coming down nearly made him beg her to hurry, but he watched her.

"I've wanted to do this for a few days now. When you were in the shower the other day, as a matter of fact." He asked her why she'd not. "Mrs. Bailey was in labor. I'm sure she might have been a tad upset with you if she had the baby without you."

"Yes. Maybe." His pants were pulled down to his thighs, his boxers as well. When Rayne rubbed her cheek over his cock, he held onto the table tightly. "You're making me hurt, I need you so much."

She didn't just take him into her mouth, but swallowed around him until he was past the tight muscles at the back of her throat. Throwing back his head, he tried to think about anything but what she was doing at the moment, wanting this to last as long as he could. But then she cupped his balls, rolling them into her warm palm gently.

"Rayne, please." He begged her, not even sure what he was begging for, but it mattered little. She sucked his cock, fondling his balls until he thought for sure that he was going to die. Not just from the pain of not coming, but his heart wasn't going to be able to take much more of it. "Baby, I'm going to —"

195

A final twist, the tiniest abuse to his balls, brought him over the edge, down the canyon, and over the rainbow in seconds. As he continued to spill himself down her throat, his body hardened again. His need, even after coming that much, seemed to triple with the need to come again. This time, deep within her.

Jerking her up from the floor, he knew that he was being less than gentlemanly. His need was out of control and there wasn't anything to slow him down. Even as his wolf snarled at him to take her, he knew that he had to taste her as well. Letting his wolf take him as soon as she was spread out on the table for him, his wolf lunged at her heat and fucked her hard with his tongue.

Her screams were like music to his ears. She came so many times that her juices were flowing freely, her body limp with it. Taking his body back, he stood over her, his cock at her entrance, and commanded that she watch him.

As soon as their eyes connected, he slammed into her, his cock buried so deeply within her that she bowed up from the table. And when he fucked her, hard pounding strokes that moved his table, he held her to him, his fingers digging deeply into her skin.

"Come." She did so, her entire being seeming to come with it. And when he felt his own release coming upon him, he leaned over her and bit hard on her nipple. Tasting her blood, need, and wolf gave him the last push over the edge once more until he had no choice but to fall on her.

Moving was difficult. His knees were wobbly and his heart was still racing. Staggering over to his chair, he sat there for a few minutes before starting to laugh. And once he started, he wasn't sure he'd be able to stop. They had not only ruined their clothing in their rush, but the room looked like a bomb had gone off in it. A few of his supplies were dumped too, and crushed.

"You sure know how to make a girl feel good." He nodded to her and put out his hands to have her come sit on his lap. "I can't. Christ, I feel like I've been hung out to dry on a windy day. What got into you?"

"You. Or better yet, I got into you. Anytime you want to come here and take me like that, Rayne, you go right ahead. That was fantastic." She asked him if they were still going to the woods. "Yes, but I think we should take both cars now. I was going to seduce you on the way there, but I'm too exhausted now."

"Me too, and I have nothing to wear." He gave her his shirt that wasn't in too bad of shape, and he pulled his pants on to go to his car. There was always something in it to wear. Coming back in, he saw that she had on his shirt and a pair of his scrubs that were too big. "I guess I need to be better prepared now too."

"Yes." Handing her the bag to let her pick what she wanted, Rayne ended up with his T-shirt on, as well as the scrubs. He pulled on his socks and another shirt and sat in the chair. "I was wondering about what we talked about last night. The little girl, Penny. Do you suppose that someone will come forward eventually?"

"No, she's pretty much alone. Her mom and I went over the names that she could remember in her family. Sometimes you'll come to realize that they can't always remember names as well as they do faces. Anyway, she doesn't have anyone living that can care for her. Besides, I think Xander and her are making a good start on this. She's already calling him

197

Dad, believe it or not." He pulled on his shoes and leaned back to watch her pull hers on. "I heard from a man by the name of Wayne. I think his first name was Gilbert. Anyway, he thinks he might have found the grandson or great-grandson of Owen's treasures. He's going to have dinner with him in a few days."

"Good. The sooner we can get this figured out as a family, the better it will be on him. He's overwhelmed, but I think he's doing better now that someone else knows what he's found. Did he tell you that some of the tea cups that he found are one of a kind? That they'd been made especially for Birdie?" Rayne asked him what he was going to do with them. "I'm not sure. My mom wants a couple of them and he said she could have them, but she wants to purchase them. For what they're worth. I don't think that's going to go over well, do you?"

"No, I think, however, that your mom will win and she'll pay for the cups." When she was near her car, he watched her fuss with the trim around the door before she continued. "I have all the money that was found at my dad's house. I was wondering if you could help me set up a trust fund for the pack to use for education."

"Yes, I can do that. I bet that the rest of us would contribute to it as well." She nodded, still appearing distracted. "Rayne?"

"He's dead. I mean, I know you're aware of that, but my dad is dead and I never got any answers. None. And now that my mom is gone, I don't know what happened that day other than he shoved her down the stairs because I was sleeping in the next room." He didn't answer her...he wasn't sure what to say, to be honest. "I know that it matters little, really, but it would be nice to know why he even bothered with me if he didn't want me around."

"He's a fool." She nodded. "Let's go home and we'll talk about it. You don't want to stand out here and do it, do you?"

"No. Yes, I'd like to go home and play in the yard with you." He smiled when she did. "Then later, I'd like to just snuggle on the couch and let you hold me. I need that."

"I'd like that very much too. I'll see you at home. All right?" She said he would. Starting his car, Gabe felt better than he had in months. Years probably.

~~~

Blaine was waiting for someone to help him. For two days now he'd been wandering around trying to get one person to listen to him. Just yesterday he'd seen that husband of Rayne's coming out of his offices, but Rayne had been with him. For some reason, he thought that if he had approached her then, she would have banished him. Like he was nothing to her.

He wasn't keen on people ignoring him. Then like a bolt of lightning, he realized they weren't, but instead just not seeing him. He was fucking dead. But the kick in the ass about that was, he couldn't even enjoy bothering anyone because he was fucking dead.

Just as he was going to start walking around again, he saw her. Rayne was coming out of the bank, and she looked happy.

"I'm fucking dead." She told him she knew that. "And you've not told me how that can be fixed. I want you to fix it so that I'm with the living. The dead are boring, and they don't want to have anything to do with me."

"I think that's more your fault than theirs. You can only see people when you're dead that you had something to do with as a living person. Anyone that knows you knows what

199

an asshole you are. Thus, they're avoiding you." She smiled at him, but he had a feeling it wasn't friendly, and he'd done nothing to her. "You're being a nuisance, Blaine, and pissing them off. Behave, or I'll be forced to reckon with you."

"Reckon with me? I don't think so. This is what you're supposed to do, help me." She told him that she had helped him. "How? I'm still dead, aren't I? And I've been looking for my dad…what did you do with him?"

"He's moved on." Blaine knew what that meant, but he didn't care for it any more than he did being fucking dead. "You keep thinking that. That you're fucking dead. You do know that you're just dead, and fucking is done for you. There is no fucking anything for you."

"Why not?" Rayne got into her car and he joined her there. It was something that he had accidently figured out when he'd been walking along and a truck had driven through him. "Why can't I have sex on this side? Not that it matters because you're going to fix me soon, but why the fuck not?"

"You have no blood." He didn't understand that either until she looked down at his lap. "Without blood, you can't get hard. Without getting hard, no sex. And not that it matters, but there is no one that will have it with you that you know. And as I pointed out before, no one likes you."

He didn't think that was quite right, but didn't argue with her about it now. Blaine had more important matters to think about. Like his house.

"There is construction going on at my house. Why?" She told him that he was dead. "For now. I want them out of my home. I'm going to be moving back in there when I get you to do your job."

"My job is to help you deal with your death, keep you in

line, and to make sure that you have all that you need." He said that he needed to be not fucking dead. "Yes, so you've said, several hundred times now. But you are dead, and now you have to deal with it. I'm going home. You know that you can't go there. So, say whatever it is you want to say that does not have anything to do with you being fucking dead, and we'll part ways."

"You are going to bring me back, Rayne. I swear to Christ, if you don't, then I'm going to make your life a living hell. I can. I've been hanging out with some people that can make it happen, and then what will it be for you?" She told him to try. "I will. You're going to regret this."

She turned and looked at him. He could see something that he'd not noticed before, a strength or something. Like she knew a great deal more than he ever would or — and this is what scared him, he thought — she was going to hurt him in ways that he could never imagine coming back from.

"Do you want to be sent on?" He shook his head. "Then I would suggest that you find something to do. Either watch the sun rise or go down. Go to a porn store and hang out there. Anything but what you are currently doing."

"I don't want to be dead." She huffed at him and he watched her pull into traffic, what little there was. This place was just as bad as he'd thought it would be. He wished he'd died somewhere fun. Even Columbus would have been better than this little place called Zanesville of all things. "When can you meet with me to get this process started? I have a lot of things that are just hanging, and I need to get to breathing again so — "

"Look. You're dead. Or as you like to say it, fucking dead. There is no coming back from it. You were shot once in the head two weeks ago, and now you are nothing more than worm food. You will follow the rules of your kind or you'll be sent away. You have really started to get on my last nerve with this shit. You. Are. Dead. Got it?" He nodded then opened his mouth, but she put up her hand. "Dead. You are dead, and not going to ever breathe, fuck, eat, or anything ever again. I am not kidding. Just stop."

He found himself standing in front of his house again. Well, it was his father's house, but it should have been his when his daddy died. Instead there were people working on it.

Blaine watched as they started pulling out furniture, some of his dad's things that he'd paid a great deal of money for. His father had been excited over each thing that he'd gotten for his house, but Blaine had never cared for it. Now here Blaine was fucking dead, and not able to tell them that he wanted those things left alone.

"You keep that thinking up and you'll be sorry." He looked over at the man who sat down beside him. He knew he was dead too, but he was speaking to him. "You and me, we had a thing once. You were supposed to pick up cash for me and bring it to my home. Instead, you robbed me one night and killed me and my family. Not that I care what happens to you now, but you keep fucking with that woman and you're going to be banished."

"How hard can that be?" He told him it was the land of the unliving. "I don't know if you know this or not, but neither of us are living."

"It's a bad place to go. You got nothing to do all day and no one to talk to. Not that many want to be associated with you, but I've been here a long time, and it's nice at times to speak to someone about things." Blaine told him he didn't care. "You'd better. It can get mighty lonely without anything."

"I don't care. I'm going to be coming back soon anyway." He asked him what he meant. "I'm going to be brought back to life soon. I'm not supposed to be dead."

The man stared at him, then laughed. It was the hard belly type that made him think of Santa or something. As the man continued to laugh at him, Blaine felt his temper rise. Christ, everyone was just bastards here. Taking the man's throat into his hand, Blaine felt him struggle. Before he could do much more, he was jerked back from him and Rayne was standing there. He didn't even know how he'd gotten to her so fast.

"You've crossed the line." He told her that the other man had started it. "But you are the one that caused injury to one of your kind. "You've left me no choice, Blaine. You're going away."

"I've left you plenty of choices, you fucking bitch. Choice one is to bring me the fuck back. I don't want to be dead. Two? Well, that's the same as one. I do not want to be here. It's not my time."

He felt the wind rush through him. Not painfully, but it was disconcerting to feel it. When he sat up, the room he was in was white. All white with no windows or doors. Calling out for Rayne, he got up and walked around. There had to be some way he could get out of there.

The room was about ten by ten, and ten feet tall. There wasn't a speck of color, not even his own clothing. Looking at his hands, he could see that they were skin colored, but his nails were black, his toenails too. He might have looked in the mirror, but there wasn't even one of those. Not even a bathroom should he ever—and he only just realized that he'd

203

not had to go—but if he did, there wasn't one to use.

Pounding on the walls did nothing. No sound emitted from his hard work. As he shouted at the top of his lungs about how much he hated her and that she was going to pay, he realized that he might have made her mad about something and changed his tune. Now he was begging her for forgiveness. Anything to get out of this sterile environment.

"Come on, Rayne. You don't want to do this to me. I'm not going to bother you anymore about getting my life back. Even though I know you can do it." Nothing. Not even a whisper of sound. "Rayne? Where have you put me and how long will I be here? I was just pissed off at him for laughing. You can understand that. Come on, come and get me out of here."

He was sitting on the floor, staring at nothing because there wasn't anything to look at, when he thought that she might not be coming for him. He didn't think he could stand to be here for even a few days, but she wasn't going to come for any reason. He was looking for ways to make himself notes, a way of entertaining himself, when the music started. It wasn't anything that he ever listened to in his life, and he didn't want to now.

After the same song, or whatever it was, played for the thirty-fourth time, he knew that she had done this too. He was going to spend the rest of eternity in this hell. Blaine Kline was in his own little portion of hell, and he'd done it to himself.

Before You Go...

HELP AN AUTHOR

write a review

THANK YOU!

Share your voice and help guide other readers to these wonderful books. Even if it's only a line or two your reviews help readers discover the author's books so they can continue creating stories that you'll love. Login to your favorite retailer and leave a review. Thank you.

AWARD WINNING, BESTSELLING AUTHOR

Kathi Barton, winner of the Pinnacle Book Achievement award as well as a best-selling author on Amazon and All Romance books, lives in Nashport, Ohio with her husband Paul. When not creating new worlds and romance, Kathi and her husband enjoy camping and going to auctions. She can also be seen at county fairs with her husband who is an artist and potter.

Her muse, a cross between Jimmy Stewart and Hugh Jackman, brings her stories to life for her readers in a way that has them coming back time and again for more. Her favorite genre is paranormal romance with a great deal of spice. You can visit Kathi online and drop her an email if you'd like. She loves hearing from her fans. aaronskiss@gmail.com.

Follow Kathi on her blog: http://kathisbartonauthor.blogspot.com/

65566071R00125

Made in the USA
Lexington, KY
16 July 2017